P9-DEP-420

The Amazing Beef Squad

THE AMAZING BEEF SQUAD

NEVER say DIE!

a novel by >>>>>> JASON ROSS

DELACORTE PRESS

Text copyright © 2021 by Jason Ross
Jacket art copyright © 2021 by Thomas Burden

All rights reserved. Published in the United States by Delacorte Press, an imprint of Random House Children's Books, a division of Penguin Random House LLC, New York.

Delacorte Press is a registered trademark and the colophon is a trademark of Penguin Random House LLC.

Visit us on the Web! rhcbooks.com

Educators and librarians, for a variety of teaching tools, visit us at RHTeachersLibrarians.com

Library of Congress Cataloging-in-Publication is available upon request.
ISBN 978-0-593-12475-8 (trade) — ISBN 978-0-593-12476-5 (ebook)

Printed in the United States of America
10 9 8 7 6 5 4 3 2 1
First Edition

To Mercer and Josie

PROLOGUE

Eustace Leonard was a terrible gold miner. The other forty-niners liked to joke that he couldn't find a nugget behind a donkey.

So he took a job as a hand on the Birdwell Ranch. That was a year after a deadly fever nearly wiped the Birdwells out. Only the mother and teenaged son, Abraham, survived. Eustace Leonard took Abraham riding and taught him how to shoot, things a father in those days would have done. Abraham trusted him like family.

That's when Eustace Leonard taught Abraham how to play poker. You see, what he lacked in prospecting skills, he made up for as a swindler.

One night, as the two of them sat by a campfire, Eustace Leonard brought out a new deck of cards. They played for nickels, to start. Abraham lost every hand.

They bet half-dollar coins, then dollars. Abraham kept losing. He ran out of money and started betting IOUs, which Eustace Leonard quickly swept up. Abraham threw more and more IOUs into the pot. Before the sun rose over McConnell Butte, he owed more than the ranch was worth.

Of course, Abraham never stood a chance. Eustace Leonard had marked the cards. He was later heard bragging about it in a saloon. A frontier judge, however, ruled that Eustace Leonard had cheated fair and square, and that the family could keep just ten acres.

Eustace Leonard was now a land baron, with no more need for gold. But greed is a funny thing. When he saw yellow sparkles in the gravel of a creek on his property, his mouth began to water.

He placed an ad in a Sacramento paper, and a week later sixty-three workers arrived at the ranch. Eustace Leonard promised to pay them with the first nuggets they dredged from Gold Creek, as he had named it. They worked seven days a week. After nine weeks, however, they had dug up nothing but pyrite. Those glimmers Eustace Leonard had seen were fool's gold. The miners demanded payment in cash, and that's when Eustace Leonard jumped on a Swedish cook's mule and fled up the Humboldt Road, never to be seen again.

Why do I know Eustace Leonard's story? Because today, one and a half centuries later, our town still goes by the name of that muddy camp on the creek: Leonardville. It was the man's biggest con.

There's a moral in there somewhere, but I'm not going to figure out what it is.

This isn't an English paper.

CHAPTER

1

To look at Pratchett, you wouldn't think he's strong.

Legs like breadsticks. Arms like the rolled baloney his mom packs in his lunch every school day. His neck juts forward so when he runs through Birdwell Park he looks like a demented turkey. He does not appear to represent MVP material, is what I'm saying. But for reasons none of the PE teachers at Lyndon B. Johnson Middle School can figure out, Pratchett's left arm is a Gettysburg cannon.

I mean, our friend throws *heat*.

That's how Hogue ended up squirming on the grass late on a cloudy Monday afternoon in April, clutching his most sensitive parts.

"I'm sorry!" Pratchett shouted, his own hands clamped down in the dark bramble of his hair. "I didn't think it would work!"

"What wouldn't work—the ball?" Hogue hissed, glaring

at the softball at his side. He held on to his valuables as if someone were coming to steal them.

Stupidball games always ended badly.

Last time me and my three friends Hogue, Jared, and Pratchett played it, we took out a yellow baby stroller. Luckily the baby wasn't in it, because the stroller did a complete one-and-a-half somersault and landed upside-down, one wheel rolling in the air. The mom rushed to the scene in a few long steps, leaving her baby dangling in the swing.

"What are you boys even *doing*?" she shrieked. "Why were you running *backwards*?"

"Because the score's tied," Pratchett had said, wiping stray blades of grass from his face. Pratchett loved to explain things, especially to grown-ups. "See, if there's a tie at the six-minute mark we have a backwards sprint from the big tree to the trash can." Pratchett pointed out these important field markers as he spoke. "And the loser has to do cartwheels—*not* roundoffs—"

"I don't care!" the mom shouted, cutting him off.

"Then why'd you ask?" Hogue said.

The time before that, the Birdwell Park groundskeeper turned on the sprinklers right when Jared and I were starting the extra-point bicycle joust. A jet of water shot into my left eye and I veered into a pile of gravel that was sitting there for some reason.

You can add the groundskeeper to the list of people I'm pretty sure don't like us.

This time it was Hogue and his unfortunate package.

"You okay?" I asked, putting a hand on Hogue's shoulder. I hated seeing him this way. Hogue's clowning skills were legendary. He could turn anything into a laugh. Mr. Easton, our science teacher, once called him "the funniest kid I've ever been this annoyed at."

Hogue pushed himself to his feet.

He shouted in an impossibly high falsetto: "I feel great!"

He chirped it out like a squeaky balloon, shoving a fist in the air for punctuation. Now Hogue was standing while the rest of Beef Squad (that's our name—I'll explain later) writhed on the grass in laughter.

Stupidball never ended well, but whatever disaster it led to was usually hilarious.

Hogue wasn't done.

"I'm ready to take on the world!" he peeped. "Nothing's gonna keep me down, ya hear? I'm going straight to the top, buster! Next stop, the big time!"

He held the goalkeeper's tennis racquet up in triumph, like the gold guy on top of a trophy. My tears were soaking the grass with dangerous levels of saline when a much lower voice boomed from the parking lot.

"Hey, look! It's Butt Squad!"

Scott Dekker had found us.

He rolled silently across the grass toward us. As usual, Roger Denton and Eric Bullock huffed along on foot behind him.

If we didn't already hate Scott Dekker for treating us like insects he could squish at will, we would have to hate him for his electric minibike. It was so sweet, so fast, and *so* illegal.

"What are you Butt Squadders doing?" he said. "Getting romantic with the gophers? They're probably the only thing you'll get with."

Scott Dekker wasn't wearing his Oakland A's baseball cap that evening, but his hair was dented all around the hatband line, waiting for its return. His eyes were the color of a lime Popsicle melted onto asphalt. His ears and neck were pastrami red, like he'd been running to keep up with himself. At his collar I could see the tips of the spider's front legs— the only real tattoo at our school.

With one sneakered foot he pushed out the kickstand and then rose from the bike's streamlined seat. By now my friends and I were on our feet, facing Scott's crew in a loose nonformation. It was a staggered arrangement ensuring that, should violence erupt, our numerical advantage would be utterly wasted. Not that I was expecting a fight.

This encounter would be about humiliation.

"Look at you guys," Scott said. "My gecko takes more substantial craps than you."

"You have a gecko?" Hogue asked.

"From the Maldives," Scott Dekker said. "We went there for Christmas."

"Does he talk like the one on TV?" Hogue said.

"Yeah, he says 'Beef Squad drools,'" Scott said.

Hogue walked right into that one.

Scott stepped forward between Roger and Eric to complete a powerful-looking three-man front. He must have known it was working, because he stood there for, by my count, six heartbeats. And that was his mistake.

As middle schoolers, we walk a very fine line. We must be cool, but we musn't try too hard. I guess Scott was enjoying the moment so completely he forgot to act like it was no big deal. And now he and his two minions were posing like total jackasses.

They must have realized it at the same time. They tried to break up their arrangement, which was a good idea, except that all three of them made a simultaneous turn to their left and now stood looking at us over their right shoulders.

It looked like a dance move.

"Wow, are you guys a boy band?" a voice said, surprising me.

The voice was mine.

At least, everyone seemed to think it was. My friends, mindful of Scott Dekker's violent temper, tried to keep their laughs to a respectful bellow, but I heard Hogue's cackle echoing off the bathrooms across the field, so I guess they didn't do a great job.

It was a pretty savage own, because Scott Dekker couldn't think of anything to say. Instead he punched me as hard as he could in the abdomen. I saw him coming and tried to turn away, but that just gave him a clear shot to my kidney. Suddenly I was down on one knee, staring at Scott's left sneaker and waiting for air to return to my lungs. I feel safe assuming that, above my head, Scott was back to striking an impressive pose.

The sneaker turned and exited my field of view. I sipped just enough air to allow myself to stand and watch Scott plop his butt down on his minibike.

"*You* guys are the boy band," Scott said, pushing back the kickstand.

"Yeah. Sing a song to your gopher lovers," Eric said.

Scott Dekker's head snapped toward his smaller friend.

"Shut up!" he said.

Eric blinked a few times and didn't make another sound. If you haven't figured it out yet, Scott Dekker is a real credit to the human race.

"Well, have fun in the park, Butt Squad," he said. "My dad's about to tear it all up."

He twisted the throttle and the minibike's back wheel spun on the grass for a second before catching. He whirred back the way he came. Roger and Eric loped behind him, but the joyous spring in Eric's step was gone. Roger looked back over his shoulder.

"Butt Squad!" he shouted, just as Pratchett fired the softball in their direction. It cut a high arc through the sky but thudded onto the grass a couple yards short of Roger. He picked up the ball.

"Thanks!" he shouted, and left. With our ball.

They had slipped from view down First Avenue when Officer Jim rolled up in his white cruiser. He just drove across the grass like it was no big deal, elbow sticking out the window.

"Just in time," Jared said sarcastically when his car slowed to a stop.

Officer Jim pushed the shifter up into park. The engine's rumble changed into a higher-pitched whine. He swiped the mirrored shades off his face and gave us a big smile. His teeth matched the car's paint job. No one I knew smiled more than our town's youth services officer. He reminded me of a golden retriever: cheerful, optimistic, but not entirely smart enough to realize when the screen door is closed.

"What'd I miss, chief?" Officer Jim said.

"Just Scott Dekker being a toxic bully," Pratchett said.

The smile wrinkled into a worried look. "You boys not get along with Scott?" he said. "I could always set up an encounter session after school, let you talk out your differences in a safe space."

"Our differences are that he punches us," Hogue said. "That's it. That's our differences."

"Hmm," Officer Jim said. "I'm getting some negative vibes here. Remember, boys, winners never whine—"

"And whiners never win," we all droned in unison.

"Hey! You remembered!" Officer Jim said.

"Uh, yeah," Jared said. "You've said it like a thousand times."

"I know," Officer Jim said. "I just can't help getting a case of the feels. I'll see what I can do about Scott." He put his sunglasses back on and pulled down the shifter. The engine clunked into gear like it had swallowed something and the cruiser started rolling away.

"Talk soon, chief," he said, making a pistol out of his finger and thumb.

"Which one of us is chief?" Hogue said when he was gone.

"Me, obviously," Jared said.

"I think we all are," Pratchett said.

"Nice try," Jared said. "There can't be more than one chief. That would defeat the whole point of having a chief."

We were unlocking our bikes from the tennis-court fence when Hogue brought up Scott Dekker's parting words.

"Do you think that's true?" he asked. "Why would they tear up a park?"

Scott Dekker's father owned the Placid Meadow Construction Company, so he definitely had a bulldozer. But Birdwell Park had been here for generations. Everyone knew the sad story of Abraham Birdwell. It was on a plaque over by the basketball court. He never married and had no heirs, so he left his ten acres as a gift to the city.

"It's BS," Jared said. "That kid's so full of BS it's coming out his stupid red ears." Just talking about Scott Dekker got Jared so riled that he had red ears, too.

Hogue shrugged. "Personally, I wouldn't mind," he said. "No more park? No more Swimming Pool Contract."

CHAPTER 2

Now, to recap, the Swimming Pool Contract was the only reason we were in the park to begin with.

It started nine months ago. We were all in Jared's pool innocently playing Death Squid Versus Machine-Gun Shark. (It's a slightly more sophisticated game than Stupidball, revolving entirely around the battle to control the pool cleaner's two sweeper hoses.) And that should've been the end of it: four friends enjoying the simple pleasure of scouring out each other's eye sockets with high-pressure chlorinated water.

But while we dove and gasped, kicked and coughed, elbowed and heaved, our parents were up on the patio drinking pink wine and hatching a plan to ruin our lives.

The Swimming Pool Contract decrees we have to play in the park for an hour every day. Even if a dark cloud rolls over McConnell Butte and rains a biblical torrent of frogs onto our heads. Even if it's zero degrees and snowing nuclear sleet all over Leonardville. Even if the sun goes red giant and scorches the valley into a glassy crust of pure silicon, *we must play in the park*. We have no say, no leverage, no choice in the matter.

Because if we don't play outside, then we can't play video games.

I know—it's pretty much child abuse. And yet I have to respect the clever way our parents did it. They knew that if any family had tried to pull such an evil scheme alone, they never could have won. If my parents had told me, "No video games before exercise!" I could simply have gone over to Jared's house, or to Hogue's house, or even to Pratchett's dad's apartment, which smells like the litter box of the world's sickest cat but also has a sweet 65-inch 4K TV.

But together, they formed an alliance too strong for us to crack.

"I can't believe we let it happen!" Jared said that night as we huddled on his front lawn, shivering and slapping mosquitos. "We were fifteen feet away the whole time!"

"They're grown-ups," Pratchett said through chattering teeth. "What could we do?"

He squashed a wooly insect on his ankle.

"Anything!" Jared said. "Splash them, whip them with foam noodles, squirt them with pool cleaner. I don't care! We just needed to break up their little soiree!"

Jared's anger was slow to arrive, but once it was on the scene he was a different kid entirely. I called him Mad Jared. Mad Jared's eyes seemed to glow from some internal fire. Mad Jared talked more than regular Jared, with a noticeably larger vocabulary. It was like he needed more words to communicate the depth of his fury.

"If we'd splashed them, they just would've moved inside," Pratchett said.

"Then we could have started punching each other in the face!" Mad Jared said. "I could've driven the lawn mower off the diving board! If we all had bloody lips and black eyes, the party would have been over! You all would have had to go home and everything would still be awesome!"

The rest of us looked at each other.

"Except for the bloody lips and black eyes," Hogue said.

"And stumps," I said.

"A small price to pay!" Mad Jared said. "Now there's nothing we can do. It's a fait accompli."

See what I mean about his vocabulary?

"Actually," Pratchett said, whipping out his phone, "we *could* take them to federal court on antitrust charges."

Pratchett was always saying "actually," followed by something no other kid in middle school could possibly know.

"Oh, yes!" Hogue said. "Whatever that is, let's please do that! You guys will *love* the courthouse."

But Pratchett was already shaking his head, thumb-scrolling through a law-review article with one hand while waving away bloodsuckers with the other.

"Actually, I take that back," he said. "I'm pretty sure we lack standing."

That sounded bad, whatever it meant.

So began the SPC era. If nothing else, I like to think it's proven the high moral character of its victims—us. We have shown perfectly good form throughout the ordeal.

There was one act of defiance, but in the end nothing happened. A month after the infamous pool party, Hogue sprained his ankle in an early game of Stupidball and placed a call to Child Protective Services complaining of parental cruelty. But the matter was quickly cleared up after a series of eleven home visits by social workers led to a hearing before a judge, who ordered psychiatric evaluations of both of Hogue's parents, which were entered into evidence for another hearing before *another* judge, who postponed the first three hearing dates because—everyone said—he'd gotten a great deal on a vacation trip to Zihuatanejo, but who eventually heard Hogue's complaint and read the reports and ruled that Hogue's parents were probably normal, kind people, but just in case they were sociopathic liars who had fooled the system, Hogue's house would remain subject to random, unannounced inspection by social workers, police, and sheriff's deputies for a period not to exceed six years.

Like I said, nothing happened.

I think his parents were too exhausted by the whole thing to be mad. And luckily Hogue came through the ordeal in good spirits.

"That courthouse has an *awesome* vending machine," he said at school the next day, reaching into his backpack and pulling out a candy bar in a red-and-yellow wrapper.

"Have you ever had a Zagnut?"

CHAPTER
3

A half hour after Scott Dekker zoomed up First Avenue, I was finally doing what I love best.

Sniping.

Sniping agrees with some deep-down part of me. I like seeing you before you see me. Maybe you're waiting for your health to be restored, or hoping your Super recharges in the next five seconds, or maybe even trying to snipe me. Doesn't matter. What matters is you're hunkering down in that meteor-impact crater hoping no one sees you. But they do.

I do.

The telescopic scope on my Jupitarian Longbow zooms in to twenty-five times normal vision. It's the best distance weapon in the game, and I earned it the hard way: by completing Moons of Thor.

(If you've never heard of Moons of Thor, Google it right now. It's the most frustrating, tedious, impossible solo mission in all of *Dynamus*. The boss is a huge dragon with a cow's head, and he floats up and down this narrow shaft so you only get a shot off every ten seconds or so. If you can stay alive for half an hour, you might finish him off. When you do, he explodes into droplets of pink goo.

Well done, Protector!

Then comes the ultimate *Dynamus* double-cross: the Dragon Cow was a *fake boss*! The real boss is a sorcerer with no skin who does this lightning-bolt thing with his eyeballs that take fifty health points per hit. There's nowhere to hide because the door to the crashed space cruiser is locked. I could tell you how to beat the Meat Wizard, but then everyone would have a Jupitarian Longbow.)

Where was I?

Right—sniping. I lay prone on a rocky cliff face, providing cover for Hogue, Jared, and Pratchett.

In real life I was sunk into the beanbag chair on the floor of my bedroom, where my parents let me keep my Game-Station console and our old TV so long as I "did my part." That was their passive-aggressive way of saying I had to empty the dishwasher in the mornings and get straight As at school. The dishes were the only real point of consideration for me. It was already an unspoken Beef Squad tradition that we kept our grades at LBJ Middle School as close to perfect as possible.

Otherwise, how could we maintain our raging superiority complex?

"Left, left, left, left!" Jared said into the mic.

"Yeah," Hogue said, "but what side is he on?"

"The left!" Jared yelped.

We all keyed the mics to let Jared hear us laughing.

Jared responded by lobbing a mortar into a stand of trees on our left. It exploded, tossing palm fronds high into the gray sky, but nothing showed up on the kill scroll. A miss.

"Is it behind that rock?" I said. Meanwhile, I calmly smoked a Sentinel coming up the main road and jacked another arrow into my breech.

"I'll check it out," Hogue said. In a flash of bright-green armor, Hogue sprinted from the safety of their trench. He started taking fire immediately. We could see the flashes of impact but not the shots themselves.

"Is that a needle gun?" I asked.

"Not unless needle guns suddenly do thirty damage per hit," Hogue said on the mic. He was panting a little, as if he had actually been dodging bullets.

This was no ordinary Sentinel behind the rocks. Something spooky was going on.

"Do you see him?" I asked.

"No!" Hogue said, rocket-boosting back behind a house-sized boulder. His health would return in another nine seconds if he could survive that long.

I switched to my binoculars and scanned the top edges of the rocks.

Nothing.

Then—just for an instant—a yellow triangle poked over a rock. Was it a shield? A piece of armor?

I zoomed in for a better look, but I was blinded by a mortar flash. As my vision came back, I saw a line of explosions sending earth and vegetation skyward. Evidently Jared was getting rid of his remaining mortar rounds. It was over in a few seconds. A pall of dust spread, rolling over everything like a reddish-brown carpet.

But still no kill.

The sound Jared then made was . . . well, it was simply the purest expression of frustration I've ever heard.

"Eeeeeeaaaaaaaoughhhhhh!"

"Was that a crocodile farting into a trombone?" Hogue said.

"I think it was a raccoon getting murdered inside a kettle-drum," I said.

"Actually," Pratchett said, "it was the idiot who just used up ᴧll the mortar shells we're going to need up at the Luxatarian Gate."

That was true. The map got much tougher a few bends farther on. Which was one reason it was so weird to be pinned down *here*. This place didn't even have a name.

"At least the dust will give us some cover," Hogue said. "I'm back to a hundred."

Hogue jetted over the boulder, and that's when he exploded like a skyrocket. Little pieces of green armor fluttered down like confetti. In the score box his name went gray: he was dead.

"Whaaaaaat?!" Jared said.

"Did you see that?" I said. "Hogue just popped like a balloon!"

"Actually—" Pratchett said, but that was all he got out.

Because just then, two rays came down from the sky, white as burning magnesium. They lit Jared and Pratchett up so hot that I swear I could see their skeletons for a second. Then my friends burst into little pieces, just like Hogue.

I was alone on the clifftop. And that was when I saw him.

A yellow figure strode out from behind a rock. I raised my binos. It wasn't a Sentinel or a Pikeman. It wasn't a Reaver or an Ion Musketeer. It wasn't an AI enemy of any kind. It was a Protector—a good guy. I'd never seen armor like his. It flowed in elegant curves, more like a medieval knight's than the angular, pseudo-Transformers armor the rest of us wore. Most striking were his eyes: blank silver orbs. And they were looking right at me.

I swapped out the binos for my Longbow. The weapon's optic was nearly as strong as the glasses. I laid the crosshairs on the yellow man's nose and squeezed the trigger, but my arrow might as well have been a raindrop. I reloaded and fired again. And again. And again. He didn't flinch.

I was down to my last arrow when he finally pulled out a weapon. It looked like a TV remote, with different-colored buttons. I'd never seen it in the *Dynamus* marketplace or in any of the hundreds of gaming videos I'd sat through.

So how did I know it was a weapon?

Because when he pushed the button my screen went as white as a magnesium fire. And then the flashing red letters on my screen informed me I was dead.

"Nick Rhodes!" my mother shouted from downstairs. "Time to turn that idiotic thing off!"

CHAPTER 4

"**O**h, my god—your face!"

That's how my mom greeted me the next morning when I came into the kitchen. So much for the old *good morning.*

"What?" I said.

I reached up and checked that all my face parts were in the right place. Everything felt normal.

"You look like you were up all night," my dad said, glancing up from his tablet. He always read the news at the breakfast table.

"You've got dark circles under your eyes like a football player," Mom said from her chair beside Dad. "But I know that's not what you were playing."

Oh, here we go again, I thought.

Her lips were pursed tight like a cat's butt, which is what happens when she means business.

I went to the cabinet and grabbed a Pop-Tart.

"Was it an all-night *Dynamus* party with Beef Squad?" my dad asked. "Whispering into the mouthpiece so you don't wake up Mom and Dad?"

"No!" I said, pushing the toaster lever down. "This is just what I look like in the morning! It's a teenager thing, okay? We get zits on our noses and black circles under our eyes and—I don't know—mice in our hair."

"Nick," my mom said, "don't try to pull one over on us."

"I didn't play *Dynamus*!" I said. "That's the truth!"

And it was.

Mom eyed me suspiciously over the rim of her cup.

"No *Dynamus*?" she said. "You promise?"

"I promise," I said.

"Okay," she said. She took a sip, then added, "But it sure looks like you were up to *something* last night."

I shrugged but didn't say anything. Because she was right.

I had snuck out and been up most of the night with Hogue, Jared, and Pratchett, pulling a Beef Squad mission—our biggest one yet. And it had gone well! Now all we had to do was stay awake until third period. Which would be harder than it sounds, since we'd gotten maybe two full hours of sleep.

"What's that on your hand?" my dad said.

My stomach sank—*dangit!*

Sure enough, the back of my left hand had a big white streak across it. I must have missed it when we washed up in the alleyway behind the school. But now, in the morning light of our kitchen, it stood out like what it was: a splotch of industrial-grade latex.

I prodded my brain to come up with a believable excuse.

"Oh, yeah," I said. "We painted Hogue's fence yesterday."

On a scale of one to ten, I give that lie a zero.

My dad's eyebrows bent up practically into his hairline. He looked like he was just about to call me on it when my Pop-Tart popped.

"Okay, bye!" I said. I nabbed the Pop-Tart, slung my backpack on, and dashed out the side door.

My bike was in the driveway, right where I'd left it a couple hours earlier.

Every day that it wasn't raining, Pratchett and I rode to school together, while Hogue and Jared rode from the other side of the park. Pratchett had a perfect attendance record going back to the second half of second grade—934 consecutive school days and counting. If the day comes when he isn't waiting for me next to the mailbox in front of his mom's gray one-story house at exactly 7:40, I will assume that a dying satellite crashed through his ceiling and pinned him to his bed.

His eyes had dark circles beneath them, just like mine. I wondered if his mom had given him the third degree, too.

"How you feeling?" I asked, slowing a little to let him catch up.

"Like my head is full of bees," Pratchett said, pumping his pedals to get up to speed.

That sounded about right.

Scraps of mist still hung in the trees as we made our way

toward the Esplanade. We could smell Gold Creek before we saw it, a leafy aroma so thick it was almost a taste. The trees on the creek banks grew up past the bridge. Their branches created an archway over our heads as we crossed.

Then we were downtown.

We passed under the Pyrite Days banner, which announced that this year's event was two weeks away. Pyrite Days is our town's attempt to have some fun with our inglorious history. The Esplanade closes down for a parade, and there's a festival in Birdwell Park. The men of the local civics club, the Butte Nuggets (yes, really), dress up like prospectors and lead kids into the creek to pan for those flakes of worthless color. It's my favorite weekend of the year—better than Christmas and my birthday put together.

Candy just tastes better when firefighters toss it off a truck.

Celebrating our town seemed especially important because lately things weren't panning out much better than they had in the camp along the creek that started everything off.

As my dad once put it, reading the morning headlines: "This little town is broke."

As Pratchett and I rolled through downtown, we passed the telltale sign of a city in trouble: one boarded-up shop after another. Valhalla Hardware, closed. Barth's Sporting Goods, Schofield's Ice Cream, Land of Bikes—all gone. Their windows were papered over to keep people from seeing all the nothing inside.

The megastores at the edge of town were doing fine, but who wants to ride their bike all the way to the freeway just to get an ice cream cone?

Butte Nuggets Hall squatted on the corner of Lincoln Avenue. I'm sure it was an impressive building by Gold Rush standards. If you were a prospector who hadn't seen a structure bigger than an outhouse in five years, you might think this lumpy toad of a clubhouse was the Taj Mahal. Mismatched river stones made up the sidewalls. Half-circle windows under the eaves reminded me of orange wedges. The front boasted a row of wood columns that didn't look 100 percent straight.

The most interesting thing about it was its secrecy: only Butte Nuggets members were allowed inside.

Above the awning, one crucial letter was missing from the sign, so it proudly proclaimed:

BUTT   NUGGETS HALL

It had been that way for five weeks and counting. For the record, I have no idea who stole the "e" or where it is now. Just please don't look in the back of Hogue's locker.

We dipped our handlebars and turned the corner, and there was LBJ Middle School. The one-story campus had been laid out like a fish skeleton. The main hallway ran up the middle, with five corridors branching off each side like ribs. The gym and locker rooms made up the fish's tail, the library and cafeteria were somewhere by the gills, and the vice principal's office was the head.

But I'm definitely not saying that Vice Principal Hopper has fish brains. That would be disrespectful and wrong.

Drop-off was in full effect at the curb. A train of parental vans and SUVs inched forward. At the front of the line our classmates got out one or two at a time, slinging backpacks as heavy as small moons.

Pratchett and I veered around past the teachers' parking lot.

"Hi, boys," Ms. Power called from behind the clamshell of her open trunk. Ms. Power was our pre-algebra teacher. That morning she was carrying a flat board containing some kind of geometry game. She held it just as skillfully as she held her server's tray at the Giraffe.

That's another sign Leonardville is broke—our teachers take second jobs on the weekends.

The worst feeling of the day is arriving at the bike cage. Our ride through the leafy streets is just a tease of freedom on the way to these six iron racks surrounded by a chain-link fence.

You fly into the bike cage like a bird but walk out like a lizard.

A few dozen of our classmates were hunched over their bikes, affixing locks. Pratchett and I found open spots and did the same.

I don't think other kids like the place any more than I do. Things turn nasty here.

"Nice bike, *Brat*chett," Mo Stephens's mouth said. I say his mouth said it because everything north of there was cast in deep shadow by the brim of his cap. Mo lived in a cloud of negativity that occasionally rained abuse down on us. But he was far too mellow to ever pose a Scott Dekker–style threat. Today the target of that negativity was Pratchett's red-and-white cruiser, a bike he'd carefully painted himself last summer.

"Thanks," Pratchett said, unfazed. I've got to hand it to my friend: insults bounce off him like rubber bands. Sometimes it's like he's reporting from another dimension the rest of us are too dumb to see. A dimension where Mo Stephens hardly exists.

Or maybe Pratchett's head was just full of bees because we'd been up all night rigging an epic prank for third period.

The wall by the back doors of the school is smudged with dark crescents from years and years' worth of skateboarding tricks. It's the spot where Jesse Concepción landed a near-impossible trick: the falling tall-wall stalled Pall Mall. The video's online.

Pratchett and I waited by the smudges for Jared and Hogue. Our schoolmates filed past us in ones and twos. I was excited about third period, but Beef Squad has a strict rule against talking in public about any of our missions. That rule is why we've never been caught, and never will be. Instead, Pratchett and I talked about the strange intruder in our video game the night before. We'd started calling him the Yellow Knight.

"I think he's an Easter egg," I said. "One of us must have triggered him. Some combination one of us hit without knowing it. Or maybe it was when I jumped up onto the cliff."

That was my pride talking. Getting up to that position had been nearly impossible.

"Actually," Pratchett said, "there are only four Easter eggs on that mission, and they're all past the Gate."

"According to who?" I said.

"UnicornKisses," Pratchett said.

I nodded. UnicornKisses was the unofficial mayor of *Dynamus*. His gameplay videos were practically our Bible.

"*You* talked to UnicornKisses?" Hogue said, approaching us from the bike cage, Jared following a step behind. "Does he like asparagus?"

(It's a long story, but Hogue is moderately obsessed with asparagus.)

"Yeah," Pratchett said. "He said it's delicious for breakfast."

"Only if you dip it in jelly," Hogue said.

Finally we were all back together. Jared looked in even worse shape than me.

"How you doing?" I said to him.

Hogue answered for him: "I had to wake him up."

"I was *awake*!" Jared said. "I was just resting my eyes."

"In bed? With your pajamas still on?" Hogue said.

"Okay," I said, "so what was that yellow hypebeast who blasted us all into cornflakes?"

"Isn't it obvious?" Jared said. "Someone's cheating."

Boom.

"Oh, here we go!" I said.

Video gamers talk about cheaters the way the Pilgrims

used to talk about witches. Whenever something bad happens, you can always blame a cheater. And best of all, you can never be proven wrong. Of course, you can never be proven *right*, either, but that doesn't matter to people as much as you might think.

"No way," I said. "No one's ever put up a legit cheat video."

"It just fits," Jared said. "There's no other explanation."

"Actually . . . ," Pratchett said, to my relief: finally, someone to talk sense. "Jared's analysis is the best."

"What?!" I said. "Not you, too!"

"The Yellow Knight did everything a cheating player would do and nothing a Sentinel or an Easter egg would do," Pratchett said. "What kind of things would you do if you could do anything? You'd design custom armor no one else has. You'd make yourself impervious to other players' attacks. You'd definitely invade private missions where no one would expect to find you—"

"Hello!" Jared said.

"And you'd create a new weapon of unparalleled power," Pratchett said. "But you'd want it to be more than just powerful. You'd want it to be . . ."

He looked around, as if drawing inspiration from our dismal surroundings.

". . . *obnoxious,*" he said.

"For instance?" Jared said, looking at me triumphantly. He was making me finish his argument for him.

I sighed in defeat. "A TV remote."

CHAPTER 5

Mr. Easton, our science teacher, is the greatest, smartest, funnest, funniest, *best* teacher in the entire history of middle school.

He doesn't just understand science; he understands us. Seventh graders, I mean. I think he might even *like* us.

Once, he noticed Hogue ignoring his quiz sheet and staring into the terrarium, home of Lulu the bearded dragon.

"Give it up, Hogue," Mr. Easton said, his eyes locked on our friend. "I've sworn Lulu to secrecy. Though it's true she knows a lot more about the water cycle than you do."

If Mr. Easton enjoyed the laughter that filled the room, he didn't show any sign of it. He kept staring Hogue down. With his mustache and bushy eyebrows, he looked like a terrier on the hunt.

Hogue, meanwhile, grinned like he'd told the joke himself. Mr. Easton's ribbing had that effect. You felt like were in on it, especially if you were the one he was burning.

And while his jokes were funny, his lessons were just plain *fun*.

"Do you know what this is?" he asked us one morning, holding up a beaker of what looked like molten silver.

"Mercury?" Pratchett said.

If Pratchett's voice held any hint of doubt, it wasn't because he didn't know. We just weren't used to teachers pulling out cups of heavy metal.

But Mr. Easton was just getting started. He poured drops of it right into our hands. We traded the quicksilver from palm to palm, feeling its bizarre weight. For kids who don't even get to ride our bikes without helmets, having a teacher trust us with blobs of toxic contamination felt pretty good.

Then Mr. Easton collected the mercury back into a beaker, dug around in his desk drawer, and held up a lead fishing weight.

"Who thinks it'll sink?" he asked. Most of us raised our hands.

"Wanna bet?" Mr. Easton said, his eyes sparkling mischievously.

The raised hands withered back down. A few of us chuckled nervously. But Mr. Easton didn't laugh. The man wasn't joking.

"Yeah, I'll bet you," Curtis Wannamaker finally said.

Mr. Easton made Curtis lay his cash on the lab table—a five-dollar bill—and matched it with five singles of his own. Then he dropped the lead sinker into the mercury.

It floated like a little boat on a hard, mirrored sea.

"Dog turds!" Curtis hissed as Mr. Easton scooped up the cash.

Mr. Easton looked too pleased with his winnings to worry about the language. Or maybe Curtis's outburst was exactly the point Mr. Easton was trying to make.

"What did you learn?" Mr. Easton said, folding the bills into his wallet.

"Mercury is denser than lead," Curtis said sheepishly.

"And?" Mr. Easton said, pressing.

"Don't gamble," Curtis said, cracking a smile.

"Exactly," Mr. Easton said.

"So can you give me my money back?" Curtis said hopefully. "Since I learned my very important lesson?"

"For Pete's sake, Curtis, if I did that you might forget the lesson," Mr. Easton said, pocketing his wallet. "What kind of teacher would that make me?"

The day before Thanksgiving, he had us deep-fry a turkey over six Bunsen burners. Maddie Harmon and I had the job of monitoring the oil temperature in the enormous pot and adjusting the heat to keep it right at 350 degrees. We tried different numbers of burners to keep the temperature constant, but it wasn't easy.

"This oil does *not* want to be three hundred and fifty

degrees," Maddie observed as we slid two burners back into position.

"Oil wants to be whatever temperature it *is,*" Mr. Easton said. "Who can tell me what that's called?"

"Specific heat," Pratchett said from the next table over, where they were using paper strips to test the acid level of cranberry sauce.

"Pratchett," Mr. Easton said, "you just earned an extra slice of pie. That is, if your classmates can get their solar oven to work."

He peered out the window, where we could all see Hogue and two other kids attempting to bake a pumpkin pie using nothing but energy from the November sun. The oven—an assemblage of cardboard and aluminum foil—looked less like a cooking appliance and more like the contents of some- one's recycling bin. Judging by Hogue's emphatic arm ges- tures, he was inspiring the others to make some change in plan. But unless it involved setting the cardboard oven on fire, I doubted we'd be eating pie that day.

Just then, I knocked over one of the Bunsen burners.

"For Pete's sake, Nick," Mr. Easton said as I righted the contraption. "You know what happens if that flame touches the oil, right?"

Only then did he turn on the projector and show the class videos of Thanksgiving Day grease fires—huge in- fernos, unstoppable, sickening in their fury. The flames devoured kitchens, driveways, and back decks. Any place people had been dumb enough to attempt to deep-fry an entire turkey.

For the rest of the period, Maddie and I treated the pot of churning oil like a bomb, which it pretty much was. But the turkey—that was *the* bomb. With three minutes to go before the bell, Mr. Easton carved through the golden crisp of skin with his pocket knife. It was instantly clear this was something special. Turkey is usually so dry it's like eating a sock, but these slices fell away from the bird like warm butter. In the next two minutes we wolfed down as much turkey as we could, smearing the flakey white bites with cranberry sauce.

"What did you learn today?" Mr. Easton asked me as I balanced my paper plate on top of the heaping trash can.

"Oil contains a lot of energy," I said.

"And?" he said.

No more science lessons came to mind. So I just said what I was thinking: "It's the only way to make turkey that doesn't suck?"

"Exactly," he said.

I still don't know if that's the answer he was looking for.

The bell rang.

"And, Nick," he added as the class filed out of the room, "watch your language, for Pete's sake."

On what, for totally unrelated reasons, would turn out to be Mr. Easton's last day at LBJ, he led the whole class out to the parking lot. He carried a rolled-up paper bag that said *Impacto!* in pale red letters. The day before had been our test on energy, and apparently he wanted to put an exclamation point on the unit. We all formed a semicircle, blinking in the bright daylight.

"Now," Mr. Easton began. "Who can tell me what types of energy come from Mexico?"

"Petroleum," Pratchett said. "Mexico is the world's seventh-largest exporter of crude oil."

"Pratchett," Mr. Easton said, "someday we're all going to end up either working for you . . . or *murdering* you."

When the laughs settled down he restarted his line of questioning. We called out all the possible energy sources from Mexico we could think of: firewood, natural gas, sunlight.

Curtis Wannamaker joked, "Tequila!"

"Those are all great guesses," Mr. Easton said. "Probably better than the real answer."

He reached into the paper bag and pulled out the surprise.

Gasps of amazement and joy rose from the kids in the parking lot.

"Firecrackers!" Hogue shouted.

And that's how we came to receive the loudest lesson in the history of LBJ Middle School. Its scientific value was probably borderline, but I thought Mr. Easton explained it really well.

"It's a demonstration of potential energy turning into thermal and kinetic energy," he told the SWAT team when they arrived.

The cops were cool about it. One of them even covered

the top of Mr. Easton's head so he wouldn't bump it on the door of the cruiser when they arrested him.

Mr. Easton was put on a leave of absence and replaced by a substitute teacher. "Out of concern for our students," Vice Principal Hopper said that night on the TV news.

"Concern for *us*?" Mad Jared said on the *Dynamus* mic later on. "If they cared about us, they'd keep our favorite teacher in school!"

"Firecrackers aren't even dangerous!" Hogue said. "Last Fourth of July, my cousin in Pennsylvania burned down his entire garage, and he's *fine*!"

"Maybe not the best example," I said.

"I could almost accept a sub if Hopper just admitted he's covering his own butt," Pratchett said.

"Yep," I said. "This has grown-up butt-covering written all over it."

"A hundred percent grown-up butt-covering," Mad Jared affirmed.

You know you have good friends when you all understand something without saying it out loud. All four of us knew that LBJ Middle School could *try* to replace Mr. Easton.

But there was one thing standing in their way.

Beef Squad.

CHAPTER
6

The first sub was Ms. Lopez.

She was obsessed with check marks. She put check marks by our names for getting answers right *and* for getting them wrong. If one of us walked into class tardy, she recorded it with a check mark. If a lab team did a good job on their experiment, their names went onto the board with a big check mark beside each one. If she caught you playing bottle-cap hockey on the lab table, that was bad enough for two check marks.

Ask me how I know.

Hogue got more check marks than anyone because he always knew the answers to Ms. Lopez's questions (✓) and aced the labs (✓✓), but he also sang his own improvised K-pop songs to Lulu the bearded dragon (✓✓✓) and added nonsense questions to the bottoms of his quiz sheets (✓✓✓✓).

"Why didn't I get all eleven points?" he asked after Ms. Lopez handed back one of her quizzes.

"Because there were only ten questions," she said.

Hogue held up his sheet and pointed to a handwritten line scrawled in the bottom margin.

Ms. Lopez sighed.

"You mean your made-up question about whether squirrels are really extraterrestrial scouts preparing for a massive invasion of space rodents?" Ms. Lopez said. "Sorry, no points."

"But I got it right!" Hogue said. "I answered no, they're just squirrels! Wait—are you saying I got it wrong, and squirrels really *are* space aliens?" (✓✓✓✓✓)

Hogue would probably have a hundred check marks by now except that Ms. Lopez left after eight days. Some heartless, deviant, and totally unknown perpetrators taped a 120-decibel air horn to the seat post of her adjustable chair. (How they pulled this off in the five minutes between second and third periods is the big mystery no one can figure out.) When she sat down, the post compressed, as it was designed to do. You know, for maximum teacher comfort. But comfort was not in the cards for poor Ms. Lopez.

The seat lowered right onto the button of the air horn.

A hundred and twenty decibels is as loud as a thunderclap. But this thunderclap kept going and going. A blaring roar bounced around the room, stunning all of us. The posters on the wall quivered. The walls themselves seemed to sag and ripple as the air horn beat in on our brains.

Hugo Lansavecchia got one of his nosebleeds, staining a pretty sweet Brazilian T-shirt.

When Ms. Lopez finally ended the terror by standing up, it was not because she had figured out what was going on.

She was running away.

She grabbed her purse off the coatrack and dashed out of the room as fast as her sneakers could take her. For all we know, she's still running, her mind scrambled like an omelet by Jared's dad's old boat horn and Room 302's very own roll of packing tape.

(You did *not* hear that from me.)

After her came three more subs. They weren't bad teachers—at least, not all of them. But they weren't Mr. Easton, so they had to go.

Mr. Baker was as skinny as a marathon runner, which was weird because he always took a break smack in the middle of third period to eat a hunk of Swiss cheese.

"Gotta have mah cheese," Mr. Baker would say, unfolding the plastic wrap.

I would have liked to ask him about the Southern accent he sometimes spoke with. Was he putting it on for fun or did he come from Louisiana? Was he trying not to talk that way and it just slipped out when he wasn't thinking?

But I'll never get the chance, because Mr. Baker was worn down by four multicolored dots that danced erratically on the whiteboard every time he turned his back to the class to write on it, but that never seemed to be there when he spun back around to catch the culprits.

"Ah don't get it!" he finally said to the class, gripping the edge of Mr. Easton's lab table so tightly his knuckles turned red, then white. "What are ya tryin' ta do to me? Y'all know Ah'm seeing those four dots in mah sleep?"

He scanned the field of seventh-grade faces, looking for an answer. None came.

Eventually he searched all our pockets, but that turned up nothing but nineteen phones, a fidget spinner, and seven dollars in vending-machine change.

(Pro tip: teachers never search your socks. I guess they figure it's beneath whatever pride they have left.)

Two weeks after he started, on a day when the colored dots were doing a coordinated circle dance, Mr. Baker excused us with ten minutes to go in the period—"Y'all are someone else's problem now," he said—and was never heard from again.

Next came Ms. Horiuchi. She knew a lot about science. She'd gone to a fancy college on the East Coast, casually talked about digging for artifacts on the Yucatán Peninsula with an archaeological study, and brought a big telescope into the classroom. The sight of the telescope—a glossy blue cannon—gave me goose bumps, but I couldn't figure out how we would do any stargazing when third period always occurred in the middle of the morning.

"We'll figure it out," she said when I asked.

And maybe we would have. Except that on the first day of her second week she opened the high cupboard where she kept the quiz sheets and instantly became submerged in a torrent of packing peanuts. There must have been six or seven cubic yards of foam curlicues in there. (I can't remember exactly how much we loaded in.)

The result was a sight no one in our class will soon forget. Picture a perfect cone of snow-white whipped cream topped by a surprised and very angry-looking cherry. A cherry that absolutely would not be coming in to school tomorrow morning to teach these "little psycho terrorists" of third period.

The next day the telescope was gone, and so was she.

Now Mr. Varney took his turn at the head of science class. He was almost bad enough to make us question why we had chased the others away.

"Today's letter is 'G,'" he said, pointing his nose up toward the lights for some reason.

A collective sigh rose from the class.

"You will open your books to 'G'!" he said louder.

Mr. Varney looked like a tortoise that had eaten a bottle of hair-growth pills and learned to tie a very greasy necktie. His eyes were small and widely spaced. His nose seemed to blend into his upper lip, which made his chin look oddly small. His skin was pale and flaky and his scalp itched constantly, judging by how often he scratched it with fingers bent into a clawlike rake.

Mr. Varney's method of teaching science was to have everyone open our textbooks to the glossary and go down the list of words. One letter per day. He called this "Alphabetical Excellence."

"Science is the most logical of all the subjects, and we

will approach it in the most logical of ways," he said when he announced the system on his first day. And now here we were on Varney's seventh day teaching our class: the letter "G."

If all went well, it would be his last.

While we opened our books to the back pages, I shot a quick glance at Pratchett, who nudged Jared, who fixed his gaze on Hogue, who was watching a gray moth bounce against Lulu's terrarium.

On the other side of the glass, Lulu was also watching the moth.

Jared gave his stool a little kick and Hogue looked up. Then he remembered why he was so tired and he opened his book.

"'G' is the letter we'll be reading today, and the letter we'll be reading today is 'G,'" Mr. Varney went on. Ever the fan of the alphabet, Mr. Varney started at the top of the class roll. "Ms. Abbott?"

Sara Abbott cleared her throat. "'Gabbysmack,'" she said, starting at the top of the G words. "'A cave-dwelling hybrid creature with fishlike scales, a donkey's ears, and an insatiable appetite for potted meat,' whatever that is."

"Excellent. Thank you, Ms. Abbott," Mr. Varney said as a few students giggled. "Mr. Attias?"

Jayden Attias read the next word on the list.

"'Geewhizium,'" he said, raising a few more laughs from the class.

"Quiet!" Mr. Varney commanded. "I will not have the

class disintegrating into silliness as we learn about the important field of science."

Mr. Varney seemed to savor the silence that followed—proof of his victory over silliness.

"Mr. Attias, please go on," he finally said.

"'Geewhizium,'" Jayden repeated. "'The most surprising element on the periodic table. It has a truly shocking atomic mass and its atomic number has been blowing minds since its discovery in 1957.'"

"I bet it has!" Mr. Varney said, clearly pleased his lesson was going well. His hair shook half a beat behind each movement of his head. "A name like that, it has to be something special. Mr. Batchelor?"

Beau Batchelor read the next word.

"'Ghlurbeepoo,'" he said. "'A dollop of runny eggs that fell off Mr. Varney's fork at breakfast, landed on his tie, and is still there. Or maybe it's a gigantic, warm booger. Whatever it is, we're all staring at it right now.'"

Why do adults always say the laughter of children is their favorite sound? In the experience of Beef Squad, nothing could be further from the truth. As Mr. Varney's precious silence was shattered by the sound of thirty-one seventh-graders howling in spasms of laughter, his face turned purple before our eyes. He pulled his filthy tie loose at the neck and dropped it in the desk drawer. A blue vein popped out in the middle of his forehead.

By this time Mr. Varney was picking at the textbook page

with his thumbnail. The latex print came off in one piece, revealing the true glossary hidden beneath. We all followed his lead. The fake glossaries came off in neat squares. None of the underlying pages tore, which meant our information on which latex to use had been spot-on.

I gave Jared a look meant to say *Good job*.

He shrugged.

"Quiet!" Mr. Varney shouted. "Stop that laughing this minute!"

But it was no use. Students were reading ahead on the list of made-up science terms, hollering their favorite ones aloud to each other:

---

goolspud: A talking potato. Although native to the Kamchatka Peninsula of Russia, goolspuds speak no Russian, preferring to converse in Pig Latin. Many goolspuds make predictions about international soccer matches, but botanists say they have a poor track record and should not be trusted for betting purposes.

Grab-a-Galaxy: A distant quadrant of the universe where galaxies are stacked into a vending machine and sold for $1.50. The machine requires exact change, which is annoying. Astronomers advise that if your hand is skinny enough, it may be possible to reach into the vending machine from the bottom and steal a galaxy for free, but this does make you a criminal in the eyes of the Cosmic Court.

green dog: Like other dogs, but green.

groovy bacteria: A type of microorganism found in the chair cushions of dance clubs, custom vans, and teacher lounges. Although well-dressed by germ standards, groovy bacteria are not considered quality long-term prospects for infection or marriage. Scientists have determined that while groovy bacteria strongly believes it is groovy, other bacteria aren't so sure.

Grumpy Cat: A dead meme teachers think is cool. Often found on classroom walls and cut-and-pasted onto homework sheets in an attempt to gaslight kids into thinking their teachers feel just as powerless as they do.

Kids were peeling off the list and applying it to their binder covers. Curtis Wannamaker stuck the panel to the front of his shirt and stood, flexing his muscles in a ridiculous pose. All order in science class had broken down.

Beneath the din I heard Mr. Varney muttering to himself. "You kids," he said, "are *monsters!*"

CHAPTER 7

On Tuesdays and Thursdays, Robotics Team met after school in the Incubator. And Robotics Team was Beef Squad plus the new kid.

Thanks to Pratchett's brain and Jared's computer skills, we were pretty good. Good enough for back-to-back second-place finishes, behind West Valley Middle School in the Gold Country Robotics Open.

Not bad, for something we didn't actually care about.

We only did robotics so we could play *Dynamus* on the school computers without our parents finding out. The Incubator wasn't much, as far as tech labs go. In fact, it was the school's old boiler room, with groaning pipes running through the walls at odd angles and a funky mildew smell that Ed the janitor could never mop away. But Mr. Easton, who was our coach, made sure it had a row of PCs fast enough to crunch the latest robotics code. Which, coincidentally, made them ideal gaming rigs.

Mr. Easton mostly left us alone during practice.

"You're smart kids," he told us. "You can manage your time as you see fit."

We saw fit to manage about fifteen minutes preparing for the next robotics competition, followed by several hours of blasting Sentinels, Reavers, and Pikemen into itty-bitty pieces.

Luckily, after Mr. Easton left, no new coach had been named. I think the school actually forgot about us. So we just kept preparing the same way. That was what we were doing after school the day of the textbook prank.

"Dangit!" Pratchett shouted when a levitating ore car full of silver-and-purple Reavers managed to put him down.

"Shhh!" Karla Woo said, looking back from her screen. Her black ponytail wagged like a scolding finger.

"Sorry," Pratchett said.

I forgot to mention that Karla Woo was the new kid. She transferred to LBJ in January when her family moved here from Oakland. One look at her miniskirt and motorcycle boots told you she hadn't grown up in Rust County. She joined Robotics Team right away but mostly kept to herself while we played *Dynamus*. When she did speak up, it was usually to scold us for playing the game or to point out something about LBJ, or Leonardville in general, that she found unimpressive. It's safe to say we did not talk to Karla Woo any more than teamwork required—and probably a little less than that.

The task for the spring competition was programming a robotic arm to open a can of soup and empty it into a pan. Karla had done almost everything except actually build the arm—that was Jared's department. We wore headphones so she didn't have to hear the game, but she still had to hear *us*.

"I told you to watch right," I said.

"I did! They came left!" Pratchett said.

"I told you last week, one out of seven times they come left," Jared said.

"What?" I said.

"Shhhhh!" Karla said.

"Sorry," Jared said.

Hogue revived Pratchett beneath a salvo of arrows from my bow. We were almost back to full force when Jared's plasma mortar atomized the last of the ore cars hovering out of Shaft H.

And that's when we saw him.

"No," Hogue said.

"No!" Jared repeated.

I said a word I can't repeat here.

"Language!" Karla Woo said.

"Sorry," I said.

And I *was* sorry. Because there, in the dissipating smoke from the final blast, stood the Yellow Knight.

"That's not right," Jared said. He knew every bad guy on the map, as well as the odds of encountering it. "That is *not* right!"

"Tell that to him!" Hogue said.

"We're dead," Pratchett said. "We're dead! All that work for nothing!"

"We're not dead yet," Jared said. With a rat-a-tat-tat on the keys he touched off his remaining mortars in the knight's direction. They arced through the half-light of the mineshaft like fat orange comets. Jared was a Level 143 Heavy, which can do some serious damage. The stone ledge where the Yellow Knight stood disappeared in a bloom of orange fire.

Bu when the smoke cleared, the Yellow Knight was still standing there.

"Well, that settles that," Hogue said. "He's a cheat."

"Has to be," I said.

"Absolutely," said Pratchett.

"No freakin' way," Jared said. "That would mean someone wrote cheat code for the console *and* PC version? That would take . . . *months*!"

The Yellow Knight didn't seem to care what we thought. Very calmly, it reached into its utility belt and produced its weapon—the Tactical TV Remote, as we'd begun calling it.

"Here it comes," Hogue said.

Once again, the Yellow Knight sizzled us with bolts of white-hot fire.

Game over.

We pulled our headsets off. No one spoke for a while.

The silence was finally broken by the whir of the robot arm swinging toward the can opener.

"Yes!" Karla said, pumping a fist. "I did it!"

Jared turned to her. "Shhhhh!"

Karla spun around to face us.

"What are you guys so ticked off about?" she said. "Did you lose your stupid *game*?"

"Daaaaang!" Hogue said.

"Here we go," I said, knowing what was coming.

Mad Jared straightened up and cleared his throat. "It's *not* stupid," he said. "Video games are the storytelling medium of our time, and they represent the work of hundreds of artists, writers, and engineers. People whose work is—"

"Let me guess," Karla said, cutting him off. "You were exactly fourteen minutes into the Mines of Europa mission when suddenly a Super Doofus you couldn't hurt with all your weapons came along and killed you all. The same Super Doofus who killed you last night, nine minutes into the stupid Luxatarian Gate mission. And he didn't use a normal weapon—"

Karla scooted over to the corner where Mr. Easton kept a video monitor on a cart. She grabbed the remote and held it up.

"He used this," she said.

It was a perfect match.

We stared at her, stunned into silence. I was too confused

to realize what was going on, but as usual Pratchett had figured it out.

"The Yellow Knight," he said, "is Karen!"

"Karla!" Karla said.

"Right, sorry," Pratchett said. "Karla!"

"No way!" Jared said. "How can *she* be the Yellow Knight?"

"I'm right here," Karla said. "Why don't you ask me?"

"Are you really him?" I asked.

Karla turned back to her PC. She clicked open a new window. I vaguely recognized it as a game developer app. She started scrolling through lines of code.

"There was a guy who made a mod on the PC version that looked like a big armored hot dog," Karla said.

"I saw that video!" Hogue said. "That hot dog was a god!"

"I found that code on a Korean gamer board, got rid of the hot dog skin, and took a batch of code from one of the early *Dynamus* betas that someone had posted, so I had the ability to sneak him into cooperative missions. Then I had to port everything over to the console version and run quality control. That took a while but wasn't anything I couldn't handle. The hardest part was actually drawing what he looked like."

She sat back, giving us a view of her screen. It was totally unintelligible to me—just line after line of code I didn't understand.

"*That's* the Yellow Knight?" Hogue asked, pointing to her screen.

"If that's what you're calling him," she said.

"Wait, wait, wait," Pratchett said, holding a hand to his forehead. "How do you know how to do all that?"

"What a rude question!" Karla said. She nodded to Jared. "Did I ask *him* how he knew how to build a robot arm good enough to be on the International Space Station?"

"Of *course* you didn't," Jared said. "I've been making robots since third grade! I learned C++ in fourth grade! I got accepted to Silicon Mountain Camp in *fifth* grade—the youngest kid ever! That's all common knowledge!"

"Well, you're not the only one with skills," Karla said. "So try not to be so surprised when you run across a girl who knows how to do something."

This was more than Mad Jared could take.

"Do something?" he repeated, his face darkening into a deeper red. "You're ruining the sanctity of the game—betraying the sacred bond between players. It's a travesty."

Karla scrunched up her nose.

"Why are you talking like a dictionary?"

CHAPTER 8

The glossary prank was Beef Squad's finest hour.

The buzz at lunchtime that day had been electric. Kids crowded around our science classmates to read the surviving panels. Jesse Concepción posted the fake glossary on his InstaPic, where it was shared by most of the school. It already had 14,930 likes.

"Did you guys do it?" a dozen kids asked me.

I just shook my head and answered, "I wish."

Somehow, denying it was even more thrilling than taking credit.

For all we knew, we'd never top it.

(We couldn't *afford* to top it for at least another month. Between the industrial-grade latex and the special head we'd ordered for the Incubator printer, we were broke until at least our next allowances.)

But it didn't work.

"Good morning, class," Mr. Varney practically sang the next day. The message was as obvious as the brand-new necktie he wore: We might have won the day, but Mr. Varney had all school year to win the war. He wasn't going anywhere.

We traded frustrated glances.

With a dramatic flick of the remote, Mr. Varney activated the projector.

"For today's lesson, I took the liberty of scanning our glossary so we don't need to rely on our textbooks," he said.

There it was on the screen: The letter "H" and all the scientific words that began with it.

"Oh, and—"

Mr. Varney pointed to the thumb drive poking out the side of his laptop.

"It's not saved to any of the school servers. It's on my own *personal* drive."

"Hmm," Jared mumbled, a little too loudly, in my opinion.

Mr. Varney was right to be cautious about the servers. Jared had already penetrated the school's databases for both teacher curricula and personnel records. We had a back door into everything.

(One time Hogue tapped a few keys and the next week Ed the janitor received a paycheck for one million dollars. But Ed was too honest for his own good. He showed his check to Vice Principal Hopper, who quickly traded it for one in the correct amount, and LBJ Middle School managed to not go bankrupt for another day.)

I was put off by how thrilled Varney seemed to be. A

grown man shouldn't be *that* proud of outsmarting some thirteen-year-olds.

But he was even prouder of what came next.

"And . . . ," he said, reaching into his desk drawer and holding up green paper squares arranged like a fan. "I have four call slips to the vice principal's office."

"Hmm," Jared said, louder.

And this time I didn't care.

We had never been in Vice Principal Hopper's office.

The first thing I noticed was all the golf stuff—golf posters, golf plaques, golf clubs in the corner, a little green strip of fake grass for putting, holiday photos from golf courses around the world. The place looked like a pro shop, which was pretty off-topic for a vice principal's office. How much energy did the school spend trying to keep us kids from getting distracted? Meanwhile, the vice principal was surrounding himself with every distraction he could cram in.

The second thing I noticed was a human being in the corner next to the golf clubs: Officer Jim.

"Hey, chief," he said when I looked his way. His smile was golf-ball white.

"Hey," Jared said. "I thought I was chief."

"Oh, you are, chief," Officer Jim said.

Jared nodded, satisfied.

"Hey, Officer Jim," Hogue said as he sat down. "Did you ever catch the person who built the weiner chalet?"

Hogue was talking about an incident a few weeks earlier

when someone—and I won't say who—collected hundreds of uneaten hot dogs from the lunchroom trash and used them to build a complete, Abraham Lincoln–style log cabin in the teachers' lounge. The roof was made of pizza and the chimney was a milk carton. According to our sources, it made the room stink like a warm burp for the next five days.

"Why?" Officer Jim replied. "Do you have some information about it you'd like to share?"

"Actually, I do," Hogue said. "I heard it was Scott Dekker."

Just then Vice Principal Hopper walked in.

"Okay, okay, settle in, boys," Vice Principal Hopper said. "We've got something important to discuss."

"But Oscar Mayer Manor *is* important!" Hogue said.

Vice Principal Hopper blinked six times in a row.

The rumor was that LBJ didn't have the money for an actual principal; we only had vice principal money, so Vice Principal Hopper is what we got. His hair was as white as toothpaste and greased back so it looked like he was going sixty miles per hour standing still. When he departed any area, the pinecone smell of his hair cream stayed behind, making you wonder whether he was really gone.

But Vice Principal Hopper was surprisingly easy to talk to, because we never got the sense he gave his words very much thought.

Did he have a good weekend?

"Yep, went fishing with my cousin. You?"

Did he see the 49ers game?

"That defense is soft, I tell you. Soft."

Has he tried the mac and cheese?

"It's good but it's hot. Watch your tongue."

Hogue had a running joke of asking Mr. Hopper for the time. That might not sound funny, but there are something like twenty-two bells during a school day. It's impossible *not* to know what time it is at LBJ. Still, when Hogue asked the time, Vice Principal Hopper would snap his wristwatch up into view and read off the numbers he saw there.

If Mr. Hopper ever had any idea he was being trolled, he gave no sign.

He cleared his throat.

"Obviously there was an incident with the books yesterday," Mr. Hopper said. "I don't suppose you're going to tell me how that came about?"

He made eye contact with each of us, looking for some acknowledgment, maybe even a sign of fright.

That wasn't going to happen.

We had all watched while Jared remotely deleted the surveillance video that showed us tramping down the main hall at 12:33 a.m., our backpacks brimming with chemicals. We watched him delete another camera's footage that showed us hauling the books out of Mr. Easton's lab nine minutes later (including the moment when Hogue tripped on a nonexistent crack in the floor and went sprawling, books and all, across the hallway tiles). And we watched him delete the same camera's footage from two hours and six minutes later when we brought the freshly altered books back to the lab and then locked the door with our master key. In each case

Jared swapped out the footage with a looping segment from each camera showing nothing but empty hallways. We all felt supreme confidence that Mr. Hopper was bluffing.

"Nothing?" Vice Principal Hopper said. "Nothing at all?"

Hogue spoke up. "If you know something, maybe you should tell *us,*" he said.

"Yeah, we might be able to help you find the perpetrators," I said.

"Have you searched Scott Dekker's locker?" Jared said. "I never trusted that guy."

"Come to think of it, I smelled chemicals on his clothes yesterday," I said. "That's when it happened, right? Yesterday?"

My friends nodded in agreement.

Vice Principal Hopper sighed like he'd just hit his golf ball into a lake. "Officer Jim?" he said.

"Gotcha right here, chief," Officer Jim said.

He handed a manila folder over our heads to Vice Principal Hopper, who laid it on his desk and opened it. Gazing down at whatever was inside, he spoke.

"Of course we checked all our camera footage from that night, and I think you know what we found."

"Scott Dekker?" Hogue said.

But the rest of us were now too nervous to speak. Something was wrong.

Vice Principal Hopper ignored Hogue and went on. "But those weren't the only cameras working that night," he said.

There's a ride at Seven Flags called the Black Hole. It's

a 425-foot tower that hauls you up and drops you into a complete, total, terrifying free-fall. For six seconds your stomach is in your throat. That's how I felt at that moment. The four of us might as well have been clamped in our seats by padded bars.

"We noticed a pattern of incidents taking place with substitute teachers in Room 302," Vice Principal Hopper said. "So Officer Jim took it upon himself to install an additional camera in that room."

"That's impossible!" Jared blurted out.

"A camera not wired into the school's security system," Vice Principal Hopper said pointedly.

I realized then why Vice Principal Hopper wasn't looking us in the eye. Whatever we were guilty of, *he* was guilty of failing to stop us. The evidence in that folder made him look like he had lost control of his school. I felt a flash of sympathy for the guy, being humiliated in his own golf-tastic office. But the feeling was brief, because Vice Principal Hopper lifted a photo printout from the folder and showed it to us.

It wasn't the sharpest image, but it didn't have to be. It had been taken from a high angle in the corner of Room 302. And it had been taken just after 12:30 a.m. two nights before. I knew that because in the middle of the frame, my three best friends and I were leaving the room. Our arms were full of textbooks.

It turned out Officer Jim was smarter than we realized.

"Check it out," Hogue said, pointing to the picture. "That's *totally* Scott Dekker!"

CHAPTER 9

You know the weirdest thing about being suspended? They won't even let you do homework! What kind of sick school doesn't want you doing *school*work?

"That's part of the punishment," Dad said, laying slices of cheese on his sandwich. "Your grades take the hit, too."

"So what am I supposed to do all day?" I said.

"Think about your crimes," he said with mock seriousness.

"It's idiotic!" I said.

He turned to me, nodding.

"Idiotic," he said. "That's an excellent word for this whole situation."

Whoops—I handed him that one on a platter.

It was the first morning of Beef Squad's five-day suspension. My mom had left early for work at the law firm where she's a legal secretary. My dad was making his lunch before heading to the community college where he teaches history.

The punishment had come down the previous day, at the end of our questioning in the Hopper Museum of International Golf Vacations. Vice Principal Hopper said that our textbook prank violated school rules against trespassing, damaging school property, and something called "interfering with others' opportunity to learn." We argued that it's impossible to trespass on *our own* school grounds, and that none of the books was actually damaged, and that the whole "interfering" thing sounded less like a rule than a big heap of buzzwords.

"You're interfering with *our* opportunity to learn right now!" Mad Jared pointed out.

But middle school has no patience for that kind of truth. Vice Principal Hopper made the four of us wait out by Lorna's desk for our parents to arrive.

That was officially the Worst Hour of My Life.

"Does this break your perfect-attendance streak?" Hogue asked Pratchett.

"With a wrecking ball," Pratchett said.

My parents arrived together. Mom had her cat-butt mouth working, and Dad had his game face on. But I could tell they were mortified. Mom had had to leave work, which I knew was not easy. In her pin-striped skirt and suit jacket, she was easily the best-dressed person in the building, but that only seemed to highlight how out of place she was.

Vice Principal Hopper invited the three of us into his office. Officer Jim returned to his spot in the back corner.

"There's an open chair right here," I said.

"Thanks, chief. I'm good," he said.

Vice Principal Hopper broke the news to my parents.

"These are very serious offenses," he said. "They could lead to expulsion, if we find that necessary."

"And do you?" I asked.

The bony tip of my mom's knee poked into my thigh.

"Not yet," Hopper said.

He showed them a copy of the letter he would put in my file. My parents nodded glumly, stood, and shook Vice Principal Hopper's hand.

As we were leaving, Officer Jim spoke up.

"This can be a real turning point for you, chief," he said to me. "Someday you'll be grateful."

My mom looked at him from the doorway.

"Not if I can help it," she said.

Now, the morning after, my dad slung his bag over his shoulder.

"You know the rules," he said from the front doorway. I nodded. He pulled the door closed and locked it from the outside out of habit. All of a sudden the house was quiet.

The three rules my parents had laid down for my suspension week were as follows:

No video games,

NO video games,

and most important of all,
NO VIDEO GAMES!!!

When I'd gotten up that morning I'd noticed the controllers were missing from my console shelf, meaning Mom had taken them while I slept. I knew exactly where she'd hidden them—behind the paper towels in the laundry room—but it hardly mattered. Karla Woo promised that the Yellow Knight would continue to destroy us until after the Robotics Open was over, and that was still four weeks away.

Jared was supposedly working on a patch to beat him, but I wasn't holding my breath.

The school district had its own rules for suspended kids. The main one was we couldn't leave our houses. Any one of us found out in public during school hours would be considered truant, the same as if we were skipping school.

"It's not a request," Vice Principal Hopper had said with a glance back toward Officer Jim. "It's the law."

So when the five of us biked to Birdwell Park that day a little after ten a.m., it was only out of urgent necessity: Jared needed to test-fire Cold Vengeance, his homemade mortar.

(I'd like to hear Vice Principal Hopper explain how he was supposed to do *that* at home.)

Since I live closest to the park, we met up at my house. We took one precaution before heading out. Our main fear was getting spotted by Officer Jim on patrol. (We assumed the other cops would have bigger fish to fry.) Using my PC,

Jared made a half-hearted attempt to hack into the Leonard-ville Police Department's computer system to find some clue to Officer Jim's daily schedule. But he got a stern-looking warning window and clicked off.

"It's impossible," he said. "Let's just take our chances and go."

That's when Pratchett, lying flat on his back on my bedroom floor, saved the day.

"Found him," he said blandly, scrolling on his phone. "Officer Jim is at the Safety Now! Safety Forever! rally at the high school. Looks like it's over at two."

"How do you know?" Jared said.

"I figured he would coordinate with the schools he visits, so I used our back door into the LBJ server to search Lorna's in-box," Pratchett said. Not much happened on campus that our school secretary didn't know about. "And here's an email from someone at the Leonardville PD with Officer Jim's schedule for the week."

"Boom!" I said.

"Control-P that bad boy," Hogue said.

Pratchett never could have hacked a back door into the school server, and Jared never would have thought to use the *school* as a back door to the *police*. But together they were unstoppable. That was Beef Squad at its best.

A half hour later we were sitting on the lumpy field in Birdwell Park, confident that Officer Jim was tied up across town for the next four hours.

"I just wanna see what kind of range it has," Jared said, laying the odd lengths of PVC pipe in the grass next to a small ice chest. Cold Vengeance was a scaled-up version of a pneumatic water-balloon launcher. Jared had based it on a diagram he'd found online, basically doubling every measurement. We'd gone with him to the big box store by the freeway a couple weeks ago to buy the pipe and valve, but we hadn't followed any of the progress he'd made since then.

Seeing the thing assembled now, I was amazed. Measuring at least four feet long, the barrel leaned on an adjustable bipod made of tomato-plant stakes. Jared had painted it dark blue, with black and pink accents where the pipes joined, making it a clone of his heavy weapon in *Dynamus*.

"That looks like it could blow up the Light Reaper at Well of Hades," Pratchett said.

"If it can soak that trash can, I'll be happy," Jared said, nodding to a metal barrel maybe eighty yards across the field.

The only other sign of human life in the park was a work truck on the far side of the field, almost at the expressway. Luckily, whoever was working there couldn't see us because the truck was surrounded by a ring of green construction fencing. But we could hear the engine powering some piece of heavy equipment. Every so often a loud *crunch* echoed across the grass. A banner on the fence said PLACID MEADOW CONSTRUCTION CO.: OUR VALUES SPEAK FOR THEMSELVES.

"What do you think they're doing?" I asked.

"Letting their values speak for themselves," Hogue said.

Jared took a water balloon from the cooler and dropped it down the mouth of the barrel. We all got behind him while he carefully checked the gun's alignment. Only then did he twist the knob on the portable air tank, which let out a short hiss while it pressurized the air chamber in the back of the mortar.

(It was very generous of Pratchett's older brother, Leon, to lend us his paintball air tank. Especially since Leon had no idea he was lending it to us.)

Jared made a final check of the aim.

"Have you calculated how far it'll go based on the pressure?" Pratchett asked.

"Yep," Jared said without looking back. "I calculated it'll go about *this* far."

And he pulled the trigger.

The water balloon shot out with a loud *thwoop!* and zipped upward, fast at first, then seemingly slow and graceful as it got farther away. But it didn't soak the trash can. Because it was still a hundred feet in the air when it sailed *over* the trash can!

Grown-ups fail to realize just how much of the middle-school imagination gets devoted to how far you can send a water balloon. Well, we were now the kids who could shoot a water balloon *across the park*. As it meteored toward the sycamores, I was so excited I felt like I was up there flying along with it.

The balloon picked up speed again as it descended. It dropped like a bullet through the grove of trees by the bathrooms and impacted with a loud *sponk*.

Right on top of the work truck!

The engine puttered to a stop.

"Jared!" Hogue said. "You killed it!"

CHAPTER 10

"*What?*" Jared yelped. "Dangit!"

He tackled Cold Vengeance onto the grass and rolled over it. The rest of us spastically gathered around him to form a human shield, our backs turned to make it look like we had nothing to do with that loud noise and sudden drenching that had just taken place over there. Moving at the speed of panic, Jared had already separated Cold Vengeance into sections and was stuffing them into the various backpacks we came with.

"No one look back," Pratchett said.

"Why not?" Hogue said.

"Because we don't want to attract suspicion," I said.

"From who?" Hogue said.

"The *workers,*" I said, annoyed.

"You mean them?" Hogue said.

We all turned back to see two men in orange vests walking our way. They were almost halfway to us!

"Run!" Jared said.

We each grabbed a backpack containing part of Cold Vengeance and took off toward the tennis-court fence where we'd parked our bikes. I looked back—the guys in orange vests were running, too! The taller one was beginning to lose the shorter one in his dust.

Out of sheer laziness, we hadn't bothered locking our bikes. But now, that laziness was saving our butts, because in no time at all we had thrown ourselves onto the seats and were rolling toward First Avenue.

As we bumped off the curb, Pratchett whisper-yelled to us, "Go left! Go left!"

In times of high stress, it's natural to follow orders without questioning them. We didn't question Pratchett. We turned left and flew up First Avenue as fast as our cranking legs could take us.

We were three blocks away when we turned left again. Since we were out of sight from the park, we circled up and came to a stop on a block of tidy, hundred-year-old houses.

Splotchy continents of red had risen on Jared's cheeks. "Where to?" he asked Pratchett.

"I don't know," Pratchett said, seeming surprised to be asked.

"What?" I said. "You said to go this way!"

"Because we all live *that* way!" Pratchett said, pointing

back down First Avenue. "You want them to see us riding straight back to your house?"

"Wait, you seriously have no plan?" Jared said.

"His plan was 'Don't look back,'" Hogue said with a disbelieving sniff. "If I hadn't looked back, we'd all be caught right now!"

It wasn't often Hogue got to dunk on Pratchett.

"Okay," I said, "let's think. What's the best way home from here?"

"There *is* no way home from here!" Jared said. "The expressway cuts us off up there. The creek is behind us. The only way home is back through the park!"

"Great!" Hogue said. "We have to ride right past the guys who were chasing us! Thanks a lot, Pratchett!"

"But we don't have to go back on First Avenue." Pratchett ignored the shade being thrown his way. "We can go back on Oleander," he said, pointing ahead.

"Oleander just goes back to the *other side* of the park!" Jared said. "That's exactly where those guys were working! How does that help us?"

"If we have to," Pratchett said, "we can drop down into the cut and pass the park without getting seen."

The cut was Leonardville slang for the expressway, because for a year that was all it was—a big cut in the ground.

"Okay," Jared said. "That's actually kind of a good plan."

And it was—so good it almost worked.

We rode up to the corner, made another left, and headed back toward Birdwell Park. Cars zoomed up and down the expressway to our right. As the park came into view, the construction truck was close. From this angle we could see that it was actually a drilling rig. A spiral drill bit rose above the fence line from truck's rear end.

The machine was silent, having been slayed by Jared's hydroballistic attack.

"What are they *doing* with that?" Hogue said. "Tunneling to China?"

"Who cares?" Jared said. "If they call the cops we're toast. That's all we need to know."

We didn't see the workers, but we dismounted and followed Pratchett off the sidewalk. There was a gap in the chain-link fencing where someone had pulled it away to get into the cut. We angled our bikes through the gap and continued down onto the slope. From my parents' speeding car this ivy-covered hillside always looked perfectly smooth. But traversing it on foot with our bikes, we were soon tripping over gopher hills, gopher holes, and who knows what else. The ivy hid everything, so we did a lot of tripping.

"Seriously," Hogue said from the rear of our little line. "What do you think they're doing with that gigantic drill?"

I craned my neck so he could hear me over the rushing traffic.

"I don't care," I said.

"Well, what about *them* seeing us?" Hogue said. He nodded to the cars passing close by. "That can't be good."

"They don't care, either," I said. "I'm with Jared. The real risk is those workers at the truck—"

I stopped and turned.

"Hogue!" I shouted.

Jared and Pratchett heard me and stopped. Together we watched our friend scramble to the top of the slope, throw one leg over the fence, then run out of view into the park.

"What's he *doing*?" Jared said.

Pratchett shrugged. "Being Hogue," he said.

We dropped our bikes and ran up after him. Of course the fence didn't slow us down. Middle schoolers can climb chain-link so easily I'm surprised grown-ups still make the stuff. We plopped down on the other side and instinctively stayed low.

No one was there—not the workers in orange vests and not Hogue.

Suddenly, to our left, the truck chugged to life again. From here we could see the drill bit spinning.

(Piecing it together later, we decided that the water balloon had not killed the truck after all. The workers, surprised by the sudden rain shower, had probably cut the engine to see what was going on.)

Without even discussing it, we moved toward the truck.

Green mesh was stretched across the fencing, making it hard to see through. When we got close, we noticed that the fence was actually a lot of smaller fences. Each ten-foot segment was connected to the one next to it with plastic ties. But some were crooked in a way that left gaps between them.

The truck engine was revving at a high rate, covering any sound we might have made. I figured one of us should recon the fence perimeter while the others stayed put, so I got Pratchett's and Jared's attention.

"Psssssssst!"

They looked back at me. Whispering would have been useless under the engine's roar, so I delivered a series of tactical hand signals to convey my message: three karate chops and four finger pokes, ending in a fist-to-palm salute with a little head bow.

Jared returned the salute. He understood perfectly! I was good to go.

I crept counterclockwise to the far side of the fence. There, a gap wide enough to walk through separated two fence sections: the workers' entrance.

I scurried back to where Pratchett and Jared were waiting, only to find they weren't waiting at all. Jared was already slipping through *another* gap in the fencing, and Pratchett was close behind him.

We really needed to work on our tactical hand signals.

There's a moment in every Beef Squad mission when I feel our power the strongest. Don't get me wrong; I know we're not superheroes. But we're willing to see a possibility and then to go ahead and *do it*—to crawl through a gap in a fence, or sneak out together in the middle of the night, or push through the teachers'-lounge door with a bucket of lukewarm hot dogs—when people are least expecting us.

We're just seventh graders, but we have imagination and courage. Those two things equal power.

It wasn't exactly glorious using our power to find our

weird friend who'd run away, but into the gap I crawled, right behind Pratchett.

The truck sat braced by four hydraulic feet. At the rear, the drill bit spun down into the ground. A gurgling rumble rose out of the hole, as if the drill were tormenting some underground-dwelling beast. Reddish dirt lifted by the threads surrounded the drill in a neat doughnut-shaped mound, like the swelling around a wound. The smell of broken earth filled the little enclosure.

And there, poking through the dirt with his index fingers, was Hogue.

Suddenly voices came from the other side of the truck. I ducked to look underneath: two sets of leather work boots faced each other directly across from us. As long as the guys wearing the boots stayed there, no one would see us.

"If it wasn't those kids, why'd they run away?" one of them was saying. His voice was high and reedy, carrying easily through the low rumblings of the drill and engine. "Little brats should be in school anyway, right?"

"How should I know?" the other replied. His voice was lower but I could just make out his words. "I'm only sayin' I used to do water balloons when I was a kid, and I never saw none go no hundred and fifty yards."

Back beside the drill, Pratchett was talking into Hogue's ear, no doubt asking if we could maybe get out of there now, please. But Hogue made no sign of moving. He just kept poking through the soil churned up by the metal.

Jared pushed Pratchett out of the way, bent down, and told Hogue how he saw the situation, no doubt adding more color than Pratchett had.

Hogue still didn't move.

"Should we check the depth?" the high-voiced guy said.

"S'pose so," the deep-voiced one said.

"Checking the depth" sounded like something you would do in the general area of the drill bit.

We had to get away.

I rushed over to where Jared was now almost kneeling on top of Hogue.

"Hogue, I swear to God," Jared was hissing. "If you don't get up right now, I'm going to throw you down this hole!"

"That would be cool!" Hogue said, not even bothering to lower his voice. "I want to go down the hole!"

Five seconds later, the workers stepped around to the back of the truck and saw the drill bit spinning in place, surrounded by a mound of fragrant earth.

What they didn't see was Hogue, because at that moment we were dragging him through the fence by his ankles. I held his left ankle and Jared held his right, while Pratchett followed along, clamping his hand over Hogue's mouth.

"What the hell were you doing?" Jared growled when we were outside the fence.

"Being curious!" Hogue said. "Don't blame me—*hogue* is Spanish for 'curious'!"

"Except it's not," Pratchett said.

"You guys are just jealous cuz I found *this*," Hogue said. He held up a lump of yellow metal the size of a Hot Wheels car.

"Pyrite?" I said.

"Fool's gold," Jared said.

"You risked everything for a lump of worthless metal," Pratchett said as we all headed back toward the cut and our bicycles.

"Hey, it's Leonardville," Hogue said. "If you don't like pyrite, leave."

CHAPTER

11

Did you know peeing your pants in fear is, like, a real thing?

Okay, let me back up.

Officer Jim's schedule for the following day said that he'd be giving the Long Talk (as all of us kids called it) at LBJ's health class in the morning and doing something called Proactive Dispute Mediation all afternoon.

The coast was clear.

So after a relaxing breakfast spent texting each other about superhero movies, we met up for a game of Mega Stick Race in Gold Creek. It's like a normal stick race but played on the scale of our entire town. The starting line is up in the hills at the old Chapin Mine. The mine is fenced off, but the broken dam that used to power the equipment is still there: a concrete wall with a gap in the middle a couple yards wide. It funnels the creek water into a fast tongue that's great for tubing and trout fishing in the summer. Everyone picks out a stick with something distinctive about it, like a three-pronged fork, or an S shape with a T at the bottom. Something you can recognize. At exactly the same time we drop our sticks into the gap and then jump on our bikes. At every bridge on the ride through town, we stop and wait for the sticks to race by. Sometimes they all come by in a row. Sometimes one or two sticks don't make it, hung up in eddies or stuck on willows growing on the bank. But so far, every game of Mega Stick Race has ended in a dramatic finish down at Moment of Truth. That's the swimming hole on the west side of town where we wait for the champion. The winner is the first stick to pass the rope swing.

This time it was Pratchett's stick, which he named Half a Coat Hanger.

Mine, which I named Toilet-Paper Roll, 'cause that was what it looked like, came in second by about five seconds. Hogue's and Jared's sticks never showed up.

Afterward we rode to Imogene's Glen, a quiet picnic area by the creek, for an offshoot of Stupidball called Everybody Take a Nap.

I'll let you guess how we play it.

We finished up our second day of suspension with a spitting-into-the-wind contest at the freeway overpass. The winner was Hogue, who somehow hocked a loogie that blew back over his head and all the way across the overpass, then disappeared over the railing. I hope it didn't hit anyone's windshield, because that was one slimy oyster.

All in all, a pretty good day. As I rounded the corner onto Marlow Street, I was thinking that maybe I could get used to this suspension thing. Then I saw a car in our driveway that did not belong there.

A police cruiser.

At which point my underwear suddenly developed a warm damp spot.

I started formulating a plan. In my panicked state I couldn't think it all the way through, but it involved riding straight past my house, hanging a right on Meridian Avenue, and not stopping until I reached Alaska.

I could work in a fish cannery for the rest of my life and never walk into my house again. Maybe somewhere in Oregon I could trade my phone for new underwear.

Then I thought about texting out the Beef Squad emergency code word. It was an alarm signal that automatically triggered a planned series of protocols. No one had ever used it before, but surely this counted as an emergency. Then again, when the cop's already at your house, it's a little late.

I resigned myself to going inside.

The cruiser's engine made that warm-engine sound.

Tink . . . tink . . . tink.

Squeezing past it, I repeated two words in my head over and over: *Act natural.* Which is harder than it sounds when you've got a rapidly cooling puddle in your pants.

When I got to the side door, I took a look down. There was no wet mark. Well, that was something, at least.

"Nick, come on in here," my mom said when I closed the side door.

Three mugs of coffee sat on the kitchen table. Two of them sat in front of my mom and dad. The third was surrounded by Officer Jim's tanned knuckles. He smiled at me.

Nothing in our kitchen was as white as his teeth.

I was expecting Officer Jim to be there. I was even expecting him to be drinking coffee, since my parents always had a pot on. What I wasn't expecting to see was a tall glass of milk, and the LBJ Middle Schooler in the green baseball cap who was setting it down.

"Hey, dude," Scott Dekker said, wiping his mouth with the back of his hand.

"Hey," I said.

Somewhere back in my brain a circuit completed. Officer Jim's schedule said he was doing Proactive Dispute Mediation. We had complained to Officer Jim just a few days ago about Scott Dekker's bullying.

He was proactively mediating *us*!

I wondered if it was too late to keep riding to Alaska.

My dad stood up.

"Take my chair, son," he said.

I crossed the room on legs that felt like someone else's.

"You know Scott and Officer Jim?" my mom said as I sat down.

"Yep," I said.

"Isn't it nice they came by to talk?" she said. She sounded like she wasn't sure herself.

"I told him you only left the house after school hours ended," my dad said with an edge to his voice. "Isn't that right?"

I nodded. "Yep."

"As I told your folks, Nick," Officer Jim said, "my job is really to prevent problems from happening in the first place. So sometimes I'm doing stuff like I did the other day." Meaning busting Beef Squad with a private surveillance camera in Mr. Easton's room. "But most of the time, it's this."

"And what is *this*?" Mom said.

"Really, it's about patterns," Officer Jim said. "We all get into patterns, right? But the question is, what direction is it circling? Is it a pattern that will circle to success and fulfillment for you and for the community? Or is it a pattern in the opposite orbit?"

I nodded like I totally understood.

"Do you want to tell us what you've been experiencing?" my dad asked me.

"You mean, my pattern's orbit?" I asked.

"Just tell us how you're feeling," my mom said.

"No wrong answers," Officer Jim said. "This is a safe space."

I actually looked over to Scott Dekker for help. He raised his eyebrows and gave a little shrug: *Don't look at me, dude.*

I took a deep breath.

"My pattern," I said, "is an elongated . . . cucumber shape?"

"Really?" my mom said.

"Right on!" Officer Jim said. "That sounds promising. I hope you're right."

My mom rolled her eyes.

Officer Jim nodded to my parents, looking satisfied.

"What I like to do in these sessions is leave the young people alone for a few minutes, let 'em find their own way."

Officer Jim stood, revealing his utility belt in all its clunky glory. With a sideways nod, he led my parents out into the living room.

Scott and I sat alone together for the first time ever.

"Do you smell pee?" he said.

I shook my head.

"They're tripping," Scott said.

I nodded. Then I stopped nodding.

"Are you here to say something to me?" I said.

Scott Dekker looked away.

"I shouldn't have punched you that time," he said to the refrigerator.

"*That* time?" I said.

"Or any of the other times," he said. He looked back at me. "There, are you happy?"

I had fantasized for years about Scott Dekker facing some kind of consequence. Usually it involved gallons of glue being poured over his head, followed by buckets of glitter. This forced apology made me feel . . . nothing. Scott Dekker might have picked up on that.

"Okay," he said. "Let me make it up to you."

I must have given Scott one heck of a look.

"I'm serious!" he said. "I learned something you probably want to know."

"So?" I said. "What is it?"

I acted skeptical, but there had been enough surprises in the past few days that he had my full attention.

"They're going to fire Easton," he said.

Whoa. I wasn't expecting *that*.

"Who is?" I said. "How do you know?"

"My parents had a fondue party last weekend," he said. "Just some friends of theirs from the Butte Nuggets. Some of them are on the school board, and they were talking about firing Easton at the next meeting. They said they have a file of evidence they're going to use. Stuff he can't come back from."

"They said this to *you*?" I said.

"That's kind of the deal at a fondue party," he said, bragging. "I get to stay up late with the grown-ups. But they did swear me to secrecy, 'cause they know I'm in his class."

"What evidence?" I said.

"I dunno," Scott said. "I only know it's bad enough that they didn't want to store it at the school district office."

"Why not?" I said.

"They said lots of people love Easton, and they're scared someone would take the file and burn it. Then they'd be up a creek, I guess."

I nodded, trying to play it cool.

"So where did they put it?" I asked as casually as I could.

"Shyeah, right!" Scott said. "I said they swore me to secrecy!"

I shrugged. It was worth a shot. We were quiet for a moment.

"Okay," Scott finally said. "Because I feel bad about punching you a thousand times, I'll tell you. But you have to *swear* not to tell anybody else. Not your Butt Squad friends, not *anybody*. Promise?"

I thought about the cucumber-shaped orbit of my pattern.

"I promise."

CHAPTER 12

"**B**utt Nuggets Hall?" Jared said through a mouthful of green pulp.

"That's what he said," I said through my own chewy mouthful of cud. "Well, he didn't say Butt Nuggets, but yeah."

It was the next afternoon and I had just told Scott's secret to the rest of Beef Squad. We talked it over while eating raw asparagus outside the Food-E-Mart.

I should probably explain two things.

THING #1: Yes, I straight-up lied to Scott Dekker's face. There was zero, zilch, nada, negatory, no-no-no-no-*no* chance I was going to keep my promise. Not to my lifelong bully. Not when the information was *that* important to me, to my friends, and most of all to my favorite teacher in the entire solar system.

I'm actually surprised he trusted me! It would be kind of sweet if it weren't so stupid.

THING #2: It was the twenty-third of April, which is National Asparagus Appreciation Day. Celebrating National Asparagus Appreciation Day was a Beef Squad tradition going all the way back to fourth grade, when Hogue first saw it on a list of weird days.

"Asparagus Day sounds like something we'd come up with!" he said at the time.

We all agreed.

"We should try to make it as big as Christmas," Pratchett said. (Pratchett hates Christmas, since it's built on a lie. "Toys don't come from the North Pole," he says. "They come from China!")

So every April 23, we did our best.

After my run-in with Officer Jim, we didn't trust his schedule anymore. We waited till after school got out to meet at the Food-E-Mart, then used the loose change we'd all scrounged in our houses to buy out the entire stock of asparagus—three bunches. We sat around the picnic table beside the parking lot working our jaws like a herd of cattle in the afternoon sunlight. We were hoping people would see us and stop to ask what the deal was. Then we could spread the world about National Asparagus Appreciation Day: the New Christmas.

So far all we'd gotten were weird looks.

A little boy in light-up shoes asked, "What are they doing, Mommy?" as they walked into the store.

"I have no idea," the mom said, not even slowing down. In fact, she might have sped up.

But the school board news had shocked my friends out of their Asparagus Day joy.

"What evidence?" Pratchett said. "What does that mean? What could they have?"

"Scott didn't know," I said. "He just said it was bad enough to fire him."

"When?" Jared said.

"At the school board meeting next week," I said.

"Mr. Easton's super smart," Hogue said. "Whatever they're trying to do, I'm sure he's found a way to fight them and win."

"Most definitely," Jared said.

"That's the thing," I said. "It's an ambush. Scott Dekker said they were laughing about what a surprise it would be for Mr. Easton."

"These school board people sound like creeps!" Hogue said. "Do they hate Mr. Easton or something?"

"I guess so," I said. I didn't have a better answer.

"Excuse me," said a voice over my shoulder.

"Oh, hey, Mr. Obregon," Hogue said.

Mr. Obregon stood there in his green apron. His family had owned the Food-E-Mart since forever. That's one reason we went to his store to celebrate instead of the big box grocery out by the freeway.

"Hey, boys," Mr. Obregon said. "I've had a few questions from customers about what you're doing out here. What, uh . . ."

He paused. I think he didn't want to sound rude.

"What *are* you doing out here?" he said.

We told him all about National Asparagus Appreciation Day. First Hogue told him about discovering it. Jared and I gave a brief history of our celebratory traditions. Then Pratchett described his hope that it would one day replace Christmas as the biggest holiday of all.

"Christmas is so played out, right?" Pratchett said, shaking his head with weariness just thinking about it. "I feel like Asparagus Day has a *focus,* you know? A positive thing people can latch onto."

"You mean . . . asparagus?" Mr. Obregon said.

"Exactly!" Pratchett said.

"You totally get it!" Hogue said.

"You don't cook it first?" Mr. Obregon said, eyeing the rubber bands scattered on the picnic table.

Jared let out a long sigh.

"That's a topic of *some* disagreement," Pratchett said.

"It's better cooked," Mr. Obregon said.

"That's what *I* keep saying," Jared said.

"But how can you celebrate asparagus by incinerating it?" Hogue said. "Besides, it's good raw."

He emphasized his point by chomping the tip off a thick asparagus stalk. The crunch was loud enough that an old man walking his gray dog on the sidewalk turned to see what the racket was.

"Happy Asparagus Day!" Hogue called.

The man waved in reply.

"He totally gets it," Hogue said.

Pratchett nodded.

"Okay," Mr. Obregon said. "Just clean up after yourselves, all right? Enjoy Asparagus Day, boys."

"You too!" Hogue said.

"Okay," Mr. Obregon said. He turned and walked back through the market's automatic doors.

By the time we finished eating, Hogue said we'd converted more than fifteen people to acolytes of National Asparagus Appreciation Day, but I had my doubts. More than one of them were wearing headphones when they passed by us, so I'm not really sure they got the full effect of the gospel.

"Christmas is going *down,*" Pratchett said.

"If you say so," Jared said.

"If you look at history," Pratchett said, "things are the same, sometimes for hundreds of years, and then suddenly"—he snapped his fingers—"they change."

Hogue said, "Yep. We're just being realistic."

His confidence seemed to rub Jared the wrong way.

"Saying Asparagus Day is gonna replace Christmas is not realistic!" Jared said. "It's loopy, is what it is."

"You'll see," Hogue said simply.

As we scooped up the rubber bands and butt-ends of asparagus stalks, Hogue asked, "So when are we going over?"

"Over where?" I asked.

"To Mr. Easton's house!" Hogue said like it was the most obvious thing in the world. "We have to warn him."

Just then, the little boy came out of the Food-E-Mart, one hand hanging on his mom's shopping cart.

"Look, Mommy!" he said. "There's the boys you called strange! Hi, strange boys!"

He waved at us excitedly as his panicked mom clamped a hand over his mouth.

"Hi!" Hogue said.

Pratchett waved back, shouting, "Happy Asparagus Day!"

CHAPTER

13

Mr. Easton lived in a white, one-story house close to the freeway. Hogue knew the place because his mom sells houses for her job and knows where everyone lives. (I'm not kidding. She probably knows where *you* live.) We rode straight from the Food-E-Mart. It was a newer part of town, with less shade than our neighborhood. The biggest tree on the block was the one growing in Mr. Easton's backyard: a huge black-and-green magnolia.

We were greeted by an unnerving sight: a moving pod in his driveway.

"Maybe he's just taking stuff to storage," Pratchett said.

We dropped our bikes onto the dandelion weeds in Mr. Easton's lawn. The doorbell chime was quickly drowned out by the booming bark of a dog somewhere in back.

The door swung open.

"Well, hello," Mr. Easton said from behind the screen door.

"There's an ambush!" Hogue said before the rest of us could even say hello back to him. "You gotta do something to protect yourself!"

"Ambush—that sounds serious," Mr. Easton said in a way that implied a distinct lack of seriousness.

"Who is it?" a woman called from somewhere inside.

We didn't know anything about Mrs. Easton except that her birthday was February 29—Leap Day. Mr. Easton had told us during our unit about the planets. It meant Mrs. Easton only got a birthday every four years. "It saves me a ton of money on gifts," he said. But I'm pretty sure he was joking.

"It's the boys from third period," Mr. Easton answered.

"The ones who are either going to win the Nobel Prize or end up in supermax prison?" Mrs. Easton said, coming into the hallway behind Mr. Easton. She was taller than him, with fiery red hair pulled back in a loose ponytail.

"Yep," he said. "Here they are."

"How nice of you to stop by," Mrs. Easton said through the screen door. "Will you be staying for dinner?"

"No," Hogue said. "Our parents give us dinner every night. We just need to tell Mr. Easton something."

"There's an ambush," Mr. Easton said to his wife.

"How nice," Mrs. Easton said. "I'll get some juice."

Mrs. Easton seemed like the kind of grown-up who could turn a swarm of mosquitoes into a fascinating conversation starter.

The Eastons' backyard belonged to Chauncey, a Great Dane the size of a pony. When we came through the back door, Chauncey bounded up to me so energetically I wondered how he would stop himself.

He didn't.

"Sorry about that," Mrs. Easton said as I picked myself up from the deck and dusted off my butt. "He's still a puppy."

She set a pitcher of green juice and some glasses on the patio table.

"I'm fine," I said.

Chauncey's toys lay under the magnolia like they had fallen down with the leaves.

"How much bigger will he get?" Pratchett asked as we took seats around the table.

"Oh, not much," Mrs. Easton said. "Maybe twenty or thirty more pounds."

"That's a whole nother dog!" Hogue said, warily scratching Chauncey's giant head. Spit hung from the beast's curtainlike lips. His gray tale swung back and forth with an audible whoosh.

"He loves you!" Mrs. Easton said to Hogue. "You must have a way with animals."

"Yeah," Hogue said. "My mom says I smell like a government mule."

"Your mother is so imaginative!" Mrs. Easton said. "She sounds like my kind of gal."

Jared looked more afraid of the green juice than of the dog.

"What kind of drink is that?" he said.

"That," Mr. Easton said, stepping outside to join us, "is kale-ginger-apple-carrot surprise."

"You just named every ingredient," I said. "Where's the surprise?"

Mr. Easton sat, poured himself a tall glass, and downed half of it in a few gulps.

"The surprise," he said, "is that it's actually drinkable."

We all sipped our glasses. Everyone except Jared, that is. Mr. Easton was right! It tasted like apple juice, but with a spicy kick.

"That's not too terrible!" Pratchett said.

"I told you they were charming," Mr. Easton said to Mrs. Easton.

"They're wonderful," Mrs. Easton said. "I can see why you said they're the most promising kids you've ever taught."

"Well, that was before they got themselves suspended for some nonsense with a substitute teacher," Mr. Easton said. "Now their grades are falling and poor Karla Woo has to try to finish the robotics code by herself. I would say the jury is still out on what the future holds for these boys."

A hot feeling of embarrassment came over my cheeks and spread down to my neck. Of course he knew about our suspension. He probably knew more about it than we did.

Chauncy had abandoned Hogue for Mr. Easton the minute he sat down. Now our science teacher stroked his gigantic dog's neck while he turned his attention to us.

"So, boys," he said. "To what do Valerie and I owe this delightful visit?"

"You tell him," Hogue said to me.

I did my best to explain what Scott Dekker had told me without naming Scott Dekker. I figured I owed the guy that much.

"The main thing is, they're trying to get you fired," I said, wrapping it up.

"And they're keeping a file of evidence in Butt Nuggets Hall," Hogue said before catching himself. "I mean, *Butte* Nuggets Hall."

"I understood you the first time," Mr. Easton said.

"So what are you going to do?" Hogue said.

"What do you mean?" Mr. Easton said.

"You have to fight them!" Jared insisted. "Attack them now! That's why we told you."

"Fight *who*?" Mr. Easton said. "Nick just told me a story he heard from someone who will remain nameless about some other people who will *also* remain nameless, who supposedly have it in for me. What can I do with that information?"

"Kick butt!" Jared said.

"Kick Butte," Hogue chimed in.

"Whose butt?" Mr. Easton said. "And how? Should I print a bunch of nonsense words on top of their file? Get the school board laughing because someone said 'Poopknuckle'?"

Hogue snorted out a laugh that he couldn't contain. "I wish we'd thought of that one," he said.

"Boys," Mr. Easton said, "I do not take it lightly that you rode here to tell me this. You've shown a loyalty and compassion that I wish more people on this earth had."

"Mmm-*hmm,*" Mrs. Easton added.

"I'm a lucky teacher," Mr. Easton said.

I could hear a "but" coming.

"But," he said, "remember that you're not the only ones suspended from LBJ. Whatever trouble you think you're in, I'm in ten times worse, thanks to my admittedly foolish decision to jazz up my lesson plan with live explosives."

Mrs. Easton grunted her disapproval, though I couldn't tell if it was for the foolishness of her husband or for the foolishness of the school officials who'd punished him.

"In fact, I've decided not to fight it," Mr. Easton said. "If the worst happens, Valerie and I are ready to move at a moment's notice."

"No!" Hogue blurted out.

"I don't want to, Hogue," Mr. Easton said. "But if I can't teach, then there's no reason for me to stay. You saw the moving pod out front? We've been loading it up. They told me I could send it back at no charge if I happen to dodge the bullet. So we're covered either way."

"You're making a terrible mistake," Pratchett said, showing unusual passion, for Pratchett.

Neither Mr. nor Mrs. Easton had a reply to that. Maybe they feared it was true.

Jared broke the silence.

"HOT DAMN!" he shouted, setting his glass down on the table. A mustache of green pulp sat on his upper lip. "That *is* drinkable!"

"Right?" Hogue said. He turned to Mrs. Easton. "Can I ask you something?"

"Anything, sweetie," Mrs. Easton said.

"Have you considered making it with asparagus?"

We rode back together as far as the First Avenue stop sign. That was where we had to split up to go our separate ways home. We circled up in the street.

"He's the smartest guy we know," Hogue said. "Why is he being so dumb about this?"

"It's not dumb," I said. "He's a grown-up. The harder he fights this, the worse they can make it for him. They could ruin his life."

"It's going to get ruined anyway!" Hogue said. "That's the whole point!"

"It's like Plutonium Mill," Jared said. "He has the element of surprise on his side, but he won't use it. Where's his *strategy*?"

Plutonium Mill is a *Dynamus* mission that's impossible to survive until you learn to use stealth. If you hold off shooting anything, suddenly it's one of the easiest missions there is. Then at the very end you climb on a skybike armed with plasma bomblets and lay waste to the place. It's freaking awesome.

"Actually," Pratchett said, "all three of you are right."

"Huh?" I said.

"How can we all be right?" Jared said.

"Mr. Easton is being smart by lying low," Pratchett said, nodding to me. "But Jared and Hogue are correct: he's in a powerful strategic position since he knows about his adversaries' next move before they've played it. So the next step is obvious."

Pratchett looked at us with the satisfaction of someone who had solved a Rubik's Cube without even picking it up. I counted nine cars zooming by before Jared finally popped.

"What is it?" Mad Jared shouted. "What's the next step? Why do you just stand there looking at us like a sociopath? Why not just tell us, Pratchett? Just tell us!"

A police siren blooped behind me. I was so startled I almost tipped over.

With the late-afternoon sun reflecting off the windshield, I couldn't see Officer Jim behind the wheel. But I could *feel* him there, looking at us. It was almost like I'd been expecting him to show up eventually.

We bumped our bikes up onto the sidewalk, which was covered in pine needles.

Sure enough, as the police cruiser pulled forward, Officer Jim smiled and waved to us through the passenger window. He turned onto First Avenue and kept going.

"That guy's everywhere," Hogue said.

"Tell me about it," I said.

"Ahem," Pratchett said.

"Oh, I see," Mad Jared said. "*Now* you want to tell us?"

"Mr. Easton can't do anything without risking everything," Pratchett said. "That means *we* have to do it for him."

"Do what?" I said. "What do *we* do?"

Pratchett looked over his shoulder to make sure Officer Jim's cruiser was out of sight.

He had just opened his mouth to explain when Mad Jared blurted out, "We have to break into Butt Nuggets Hall, steal the file, and burn it in the trash barrel in the alley behind Hogue's house." He looked at Pratchett. "Right?"

Pratchett nodded.

"Jeez!" Mad Jared said. "Was that so hard to say?"

CHAPTER
14

I told my friends that I considered breaking into Butte Nuggets Hall to be exceedingly risky and unlikely to get us what we wanted anyway, and therefore probably not the best use of our skills and effort.

I think my exact words were "You freakin' idiots are freakin' crazy."

Then we split up and went home.

Beef Squad had pulled off some smooth missions, and I believed we were slick operators. But the truth was we'd never broken into anyplace except our own school. And I'm not sure it technically counts as breaking in when you use the key, even if it was obtained by stealth.

(Getting the key had been a simple matter of Hogue pretending to have a stomachache on the same day Pratchett had a dentist's appointment. LBJ rules require kids leaving campus to sign out with the school secretary, Lorna. Sick kids, on the other hand, have to go see the school nurse, Lorna—the same Lorna. Because, remember, Leonardville is broke; there's only one person to do both jobs. We knew she had a universal key because Pratchett had overheard Vice Principal Hopper telling Ed the janitor to grab it from Lorna's drawer so he could get into the old closet behind the stage. When Pratchett went to the office to sign out for his appointment, Lorna handed him the clipboard, waved to his mom outside, then went back into the infirmary to tend to Hogue's nonexistent stomachache. That was when Pratchett swiped the key from her drawer and headed out to his waiting mom's car. After school that day—before the novocaine had even worn off in Pratchett's drooling mouth—we all rode to the giant orange hardware store by the freeway to get a copy made. "What about this?" the man who helped us said, pointing to the words "DO NOT COPY" stamped on the key. We hadn't seen that. Three of us froze, but Hogue showed no fear. "Thanks for spotting that," he said. "We definitely want the copy to also say 'DO NOT COPY.'" His confidence sold it. The new key cost $1.29 plus tax, an amount Jared paid from his lunch change. The next day we returned Lorna's key to her drawer in a similar gambit: I faked a headache at the same time Jared came in to ask if he could call his dad to bring him his lunch. Like I said—simple.)

My family's Friday-night tradition is burgers on the grill. I usually do the grilling because I'm a middle-school boy, and middle-school boys love fire. But I might love it a little too much. I sometimes overgrill the burgers into dark little hockey pucks.

"This is like eating an upholstery swatch," my mom said at the table.

I don't know what an upholstery swatch is, but I got her point.

"What did you boys do this afternoon?" she asked, chewing her patty.

"Went to see Mr. Easton," I said.

"That's nice of you," my dad said. "Saying hello?"

"Yeah," I said.

It wasn't a lie. We *did* say hello.

"I'm impressed," my mom said. "These days your character is on the line."

"My character?" I said.

Her mouth was full, but she kept talking.

"Argh you a good perthon ourgh a bad perthon?" she said, finally swallowing. "We each decide that every minute of every day, and those decisions, taken together, make up our character. I'm glad you made the right—*aaaaaagh!*"

She made a pained face, poked a finger into her mouth, pulled out a petrified pebble of former hamburger meat, and set it on the side of her plate. Not a pretty sight.

"That meeting with the Dekker boy couldn't have been easy," Mom continued. "I'm glad to see you facing challenges in a productive way."

I nodded, choosing not to mention that I also helped test-fire water balloons from a homemade air cannon in a public park during school hours.

The truth is, I kind of agreed with her. Rejecting my friends' idiotic idea to break into Butte Nuggets Hall might have been the most mature thing I'd ever done. And I kinda liked it.

After dinner I watched a movie on the sofa with my parents.

"What did you think?" my dad asked as we stood at the sink washing dishes later on.

"It was okay," I said. "But it seems like a wasted opportunity."

"How so?" he said.

"If a French rat wants a human job," I said, "there are way more exciting things he could do than become a chef."

"Like what?" he said, toweling off the salad bowl.

"An assassin, obviously," I said. "Think of that. Get in, get out. No one would even know he was there."

"You think they should make a kids' movie about a rat who becomes a hired killer?" my dad said, setting the bowl in its place under the counter.

"I'd go see it," I said.

"Actually, so would I," my dad said. "But on the other hand"—he held up a blackened meat patty—"that rat probably knows how to grill burgers."

* * *

The next morning I slept late. I usually start Saturdays by doing my homework over breakfast. That way I don't spend the weekend dreading Sunday night any more than I have to. Since I was suspended, I didn't have any homework, and my GameStation was still off-limits, so I did something I almost never do: I pulled a book off my parents' shelf and started reading.

After half an hour, when my phone lit up with a text from Hogue, I was glad not to be a Neanderthal girl running from lions and cave bears.

HOGUE
U have 2 C this

ME
Wut?

HOGUE
Just get over here

ME
Yr place?

HOGUE
No, here

ME
Here?

HOGUE

JARED'S HOUSE DUMMY

ME

How was I sposed 2 know that???

HOGUE

By paying attention?

ME

You never said!!!

HOGUE

Just come

ME

B there 10

When I walked into Jared's room, I couldn't believe my eyes. It had been transformed into mission control. Between dinnertime Friday and lunchtime Saturday, he had printed or otherwise laid his hands on dozens of images that were now taped to his walls. There were historical black-and-white snapshots, modern color photos, map coordinates, even a big set of architectural plans with funny handwriting all over the margins. The pictures showed the inside and outside, past and present, of a single building on the corner of the Esplanade and Lincoln Avenue.

Butte Nuggets Hall.

Pratchett was on a tablet, drawing a 3-D map based on the images.

Hogue was lying on his back balancing a spit bubble on the tip of his tongue.

Jared was speaking seriously on the phone while scrolling through a long screen of HTML code on his PC. It sounded like he was trying to deepen his voice, disguising that he was a kid.

"When will he be in?" Jared said. "I know it's Saturday. But this concerns my building's security, so it's important."

Hogue whispered to me, "Jared's on the phone."

"I can see that," I whispered back. "Who's he talking to?"

He pointed to a close-up photo on the wall next to Jared's second-place trophy from our last robotics tournament. It showed an alarm bell on the wall of Butte Nuggets Hall, the brand name just barely legible: Severe Titan Alarms.

"Okay," Jared said, "I understand that giving people Saturdays off is your policy. But frankly, for an outfit called Severe Titan Alarms, that's not very severe, is it? . . . No, sir, I fail to see why *my* business should suffer just because you're operating *yours* like a noob. . . . A *noob* . . . You don't? . . . It's short for 'newbie,' which you would know if you were competent security professionals. . . . No, I am *not* a teenager! I already told you I am a thirty-two-year-old adult."

Mad Jared hung up and threw his phone onto the bed.

"These people are idiots!" he said. "They're gonna go out of business *so* fast!"

"You *were* trying to get information to defeat their alarm system," Pratchett said. "They didn't give it to you, which sounds to me like a pretty good security business."

"But they didn't *know* that!" Jared said, bending his face into a mask of agony.

"It's not going well?" I said.

"Who invited the turncoat?" Mad Jared said.

"I did," Hogue said.

"You're suddenly interested in what your *idiot* friends are up to?"

I had sort of called them that last night, I realized. I didn't understand how important this mission was to them— especially to Jared.

"I guess," I said. I nodded to his screen. "Is that their website?"

"No," he said snidely. "I'm trying to find a back door into the Food-E-Mart. Of *course* it's their website. I copied the source code and I'm phishing for passwords, but everything's two-factor."

"Well, duh," Pratchett said. "You're hacking a security company. Did you think they'd be running a free firewall like LBJ?"

"If you want to *help,* then please help!" Mad Jared said. "Don't just criticize."

"I already told you my idea," Pratchett said.

Jared snorted. "Some idea."

"What is it?" I said.

Pratchett turned his tablet around for me to see. He spun the 3-D model as he spoke.

"Butt Nuggets Hall is a very old building with a very new alarm system," Pratchett said. He touched a button, and the alarm and sensor locations lit up red. "There are only two doors into the place, front and back, and all the windows are too high to reach. Disabling the alarm is our only option. But like I said, it's state-of-the-art. Cellular redundancy, probably motion detectors in addition to the door sensors, and it's all managed with two-factor authentication, which we've spent all morning trying to crack—"

"*I've* spent all morning trying to crack, you mean," Jared said.

Pratchett ignored the interruption.

"So rather than phishing in an empty hole, so to speak, I suggested we bring some fresh thinking to the problem."

"Fresh thinking?" I said. "You don't mean . . ."

"Yes," Pratchett said. "Obviously!"

"No!" Jared said. "No way, no how."

Hogue was the only one who seemed capable of saying the name out loud. He sang it in three rising notes.

"Kar-laaa Wooooooooooooooooo!"

CHAPTER 15

"**I** can't believe this is all they have," Karla said, breaking a chunk off of her apple fritter. "In Oakland you can get a mint doughnut stuffed with lime cream."

"In Leonardville, you get what you get," Hogue said. He washed down a bite of old-fashioned with a long pull off his milk carton.

The five of us sat in the window booth at Helen's Donut Nook, an old-school place on the edge of downtown that somehow managed not to go out of business even though it was always empty. I liked Helen's for its honesty. There were no brand names or stupid marketing gimmicks. Just four types of round doughnuts—glazed, chocolate, maple, and old-fashioned—plus bars, fritters, doughnut holes, and bear claws, if they didn't sell out. The place didn't even have a radio or a debit-card reader.

CASH ONLY the sign on the register warned.

I wouldn't mind trying a fancy thing with lime cream, but I liked having a place where two bucks got you a doughnut, a pint of milk, and a place to sit and eat in peace with your friends. Although I have to admit it was weird sitting there with the new girl who had single-handedly destroyed our *Dynamus* careers.

It didn't help that she was dissing a Helen's apple fritter—my personal favorite.

"Why did you bother to get low-fat milk?" Karla asked Jared, who had the only blue milk carton on the table.

"Who needs the extra fat?" he said, gnawing a large bite off his bear claw.

"That doughnut is nothing *but* fat," Karla said. She sipped her tea.

"Exactly," Jared said. "The milk is my diet. The doughnut is my cheat."

Karla seemed like she couldn't tell if Jared was joking. But then, neither could the rest of us.

Clouds had hung over Leonardville that morning, but now, in the early afternoon, it was a nice Saturday. Karla, the city girl, wore a plaid kilt and a T-shirt made of ribbed white cloth. Her makeup looked like it took her an hour to put on. A little purse with a chrome chain for a strap lay on the table in front of her.

She did not fit in on Helen's scaly artificial leather bench with the duct-tape patches.

A sound like a distant jet fighter came through the plate-glass window. The roar got louder, punctuated by the clack of wheels bumping over the broken sidewalk. A few seconds later, Jesse Concepción shot past our window, loudly launching his skateboard off a crack in the concrete I didn't even see. Jake Gudmundson and the Chavez twins zoomed past in his wake. They each ollied off the invisible sidewalk crack and were gone as quickly as they'd come.

Once again it was quiet.

"How is it being suspended?" Karla said. "Like a vacation?"

"We've actually been pretty busy," Pratchett said.

"That's nice," Karla said coolly. "So have I."

There was an awkward silence. I drank some milk to make it easier to swallow the giant wad of fritter in my mouth.

"How's robotics?" I asked.

"Not great, Nick. Thanks for asking," Karla said. "The robot arm keeps spilling the soup. I've spent more time mopping the Incubator floor than I have coding."

"I don't get it," Jared said. "If you can create the Yellow Knight on two platforms, you're a better coder than any of us. Why is a robotic arm any challenge for you?"

"Super Doofus is just software," Karla said. "I can do that all day, but I need help with the hardware side of things."

We all took another bite.

"We need help, too," Hogue said, chewing.

"I figured," Karla said with a sigh.

"Actually," Pratchett said, "it's Mr. Easton who needs our help."

That got her attention.

Karla said, "What's up?"

I told her what Scott Dekker had told me about the file of evidence against Mr. Easton. Unlike the time in Mr. Easton's yard, I went ahead and mentioned Scott's name. Then Jared and Pratchett explained the technical challenge of the Butte Nuggets Hall security system. To illustrate, Jared spread out a half dozen of his recon images on the Formica table.

When we finished, Karla looked past us out the window, chewing the last of her fritter.

"When you guys texted me, I was sure it was to talk me into disabling Super Doofus so you could play your stupid game while you were on suspension," she said.

"We love *Dynamus,*" Pratchett said. "But we are capable of thinking about more important things."

"*Are* you, though?" Karla said. "You're talking about breaking into a privately owned building like it's just another video game mission. Like you need to find the key card to get past the gate, then you find the magic files and save the planet. But it's not a game! You could get arrested! You're already in serious trouble as it is. I can't believe you're even thinking about it."

"That's why we won't get caught," I said. "*No one* thinks we're thinking of it. We have total surprise on our side."

Karla nodded.

"That's probably what you thought when you printed over the textbooks in Mr. Varney's class," she said. "Right?"

"You mean Mr. Easton's class," Hogue corrected her. "Varney's just a sub."

"You guys are *not* the only ones who miss Mr. Easton," Karla said. "He's the only reason I haven't dropped out of our stupid school and done home study through MIT. But you don't see me on some dumb crusade to punish everyone or get kicked out of school trying."

"Wait, wait, wait," Pratchett said, suddenly concerned. "You got into MIT?"

"No! God!" Karla said. "For being so smart, you guys are *so* freaking stupid."

Just then, a truck pulled into our picture-framed view of downtown Leonardville. PLACID MEADOW CONSTRUCTION, it said on the side. We watched a woman in brown jeans and an orange vest use a lift on the back of the truck to raise herself to the streetlight to hang a banner, the kind they use to advertise festivals and events. It took a few minutes for her to attach it because the wind blew the corners around. Eventually she got it secure and lowered herself back down.

PYRITE DAYS IS COMING! it said. And at the bottom: BROUGHT TO YOU BY THE BUTTE NUGGETS.

Jared finished off his low-fat milk and cleared his throat.

"Right," he said. Jared was clearly uncomfortable asking Karla for help. "If you could maybe give me just the teeniest hint about two-factor authen—" he began, but Karla cut him off.

"You don't need two-factor authentication," she said. She stood up and slung her purse chain over one shoulder. "You have everything you need to get the code to that building."

"How?" Jared said, grabbing his head.

"The same way Officer Jim caught *you*." She stabbed a finger down onto the picture of the back door to Butte Nuggets Hall. "See you Wednesday," she said. "If you're not in jail by then."

We watched her push through the swinging door and walk past our window. When she was out of sight, we all huddled around the picture she'd pointed to.

"What's she talking about?" Jared said. "There's a keypad there! That's the problem!"

"The same way Officer Jim caught us . . . ," Pratchett said, repeating Karla's words.

The idea fell into my head fully formed.

"Oh!" I said.

"Ah!" Pratchett said, meeting my gaze with a smile that said he got it, too.

"Right!" Hogue said, tapping his temple. *"Riiiiiiight."*

"What?" Jared barked. He spun to Hogue: "You get it, too?"

"No," Hogue said, his smile disappearing. "It was just fun to pretend."

"Then what's the idea?" Jared said, turning toward Pratchett and me.

"Every day, someone uses that keypad to unlock the door," Pratchett said. He turned to me to finish the thought.

"All we have to do," I said, "is set up a camera to catch the code as they punch it in."

"Or," Hogue said, "we can set up a camera to catch the code as they punch it in!"

"Genius," Pratchett said.

"Thank you," Hogue said, blushing.

CHAPTER
16

Would you believe it only took two days? Sometimes we impress even ourselves.

We used a motion-activated camera that Hogue's dad still had from his old bow-hunting days. ("Back when I used to have fun" was how he described his time before fatherhood. "Fun? You play more video games than I do!" was Hogue's reply.) The camera looked like a little one-eyed robot. I guess it actually was. It was covered with a leafy camouflage pattern. Since the door was tucked around in back of the hall, we decided a daylight mission to place the camera would be safe and would raise fewer suspicions than riding around in the middle of the night.

We chose the next day, Sunday morning. By tradition, the Butte Nuggets were churchgoing men. Whether or not that was technically true, we figured that the club would still *act* like it was true. Sunday mornings would be quiet at the hall.

When we rode up, we were relieved to find the back lot empty. A flowering camellia bush grew beside the door, giving us a great hiding place for the camera. Jared strapped it to a thick branch and broke away a handful of leaves that blocked the camera's view.

"That's it?" Hogue said as we rode back home.

"What do you want?" I said. "To get caught again?"

"I don't know. Maybe," Hogue said. "I just like feeling *challenged,* you know?"

On Monday afternoon—the fourth day of our five-day suspension—Jared asked his mom if she wanted anything from Leonardville Bakery. Of course she did. How thoughtful of him to ask! He rode out on his bike and came home with a loaf of fresh sourdough, four croissants, half a carrot cake, and—stuffed down into his tube sock—the camera's memory card.

A half hour later, his mom brought the carrot cake up to Jared's room for all four of us to snack on while Jared downloaded the files from the card.

"You boys, always keeping busy," she said on her way out. "Even when there's nothing to do."

We thanked her for the cake.

"Six files," Jared announced when she was gone. "The shortest one is nine seconds and the longest is forty-two seconds."

"Play the long one," Pratchett said.

"Long one, coming up," Jared said, double-clicking a file.

"Awwwww!" Hogue said.

He was right—it *was* cute.

Totally filling the frame of Jared's monitor was a fat brown bird trying to eat a worm longer than the bird was. The bird flipped the worm around in its beak, trying to find the end.

"Get it!" Jared said.

"You can do it!" I shouted.

The worm was having none of it. It twisted and writhed, wrapping itself around the bird's head. The bird hopped around on the branch, blinded by its own lunch. Finally it grabbed the worm close enough to its end to begin swallowing it whole. Ten seconds later, it was all over and the bird fluttered out of the frame.

Our smiles had frozen, then faded.

"Dang," Hogue said. "That was *cold*."

"Ice cold," Jared said.

But on the next video we hit gold. A man in a short-sleeved shirt and a ball cap entered the camera's frame.

"That's Mr. Dekker!" Hogue said. "My mom knows him from work."

"You can tell?" Pratchett said, squinting at the screen.

"Uh, yeah," Hogue said. "Can't you?"

"Pratchett has face blindness," Jared said. He said it like a joke, but I think he kind of meant it, too. Pratchett's huge brain could identify every element on the periodic table, but he seemed to have a hard time identifying his fellow humans.

"It doesn't really matter who it is," I said. "We just want that code."

Jared began playing and replaying the three-second section of the video where Mr. Dekker keyed in the code. But we couldn't agree on the combination he pressed. It was either 9395 or 93695. Whichever it was, he pulled the door right open, which meant the code didn't just disarm the alarm; it automatically unlocked the door, as well. That was good news for us, since it meant we didn't need a separate key.

In the end we wrote both codes down and decided if one didn't work, we'd try the other.

"When do we go?" I asked.

"We?" Jared said. "Mr. Freakin' Idiotic Idea wants a piece of this idiotic mission? What makes you think you're invited?"

"I'm sorry!" I said honestly. "I didn't know it would be this easy to get in!"

"Oh, I get it," Jared said. "You're only into Beef Squad missions when they're *easy.*"

"That's not what I meant!" I said. "I thought we'd have to climb on the roof or something stupid! Now I get it, and—"

"Chill, dude," Jared said, interrupting me. "I was just messing with you."

I felt my face flush. Everyone should be lucky enough to have friends who know you well enough to make you look like a total idiot, but like you enough to only do it when you deserve it.

That night my parents were extra nice to me. Too nice. I think they had been angry and scared about my suspension. I got it. Was their straight-A kid turning into a criminal?

They were past those feelings and their sense of relief was causing them to overcorrect.

"Did you have fun with your friends today?" my mom asked at dinner.

"Mmm-hmm," I said with my mouth full of roast chicken.

"What did you guys do?" my dad asked.

"Watched videos," I said.

"That's nice," my mom said.

She *never* says that about watching videos.

What a weird year seventh grade was turning out to be.

Before I'd left Jared's that day, we'd planned the mission for the next night. We would meet up after midnight, ride to Butte Nuggets Hall, disable the alarm, enter through the back door, search the place for as long as we needed to find the file on Mr. Easton, then leave, taking the camera from the bush on our way out. We would be safe in our beds before sunup for our first day back at school.

What could possibly go wrong?

CHAPTER 17

Two winters before, Leonardville had gotten a lot of rain. Everything flooded. From our kitchen window, I watched a man in a Santa hat water-ski down Marlow Street behind a jeep.

That spring, the ivy on our chimney went crazy, curling up over the top. My dad offered me ten dollars to cut it back. My mom overheard him.

"Are you nuts?" she said. "He'll break his neck."

"When I was his age I was cutting metal drums with a blowtorch," he said.

"Twenty feet off the ground?" Mom said.

I didn't want to break my neck, but I also didn't want to miss out on the money. Pyrite Days was coming, and ten dollars went pretty far on the midway.

"I'll borrow the Singhs' big ladder," I said. "It'll be totally safe."

My mom relented, but only if I did the job after she left the house.

"I don't want to be the one who has to pop your head right-side-out," she said.

Up near my bedroom window, I was reaching into the ivy to find a vine to cut when I found the first screw. Lower down I found another, then another. Whoever lived in our house before had attached some kind of contraption to the side of the chimney. Probably one of those old-style TV antennas. The antenna was gone, but they'd left the screws there, maybe in case some future person came up with a good use for them.

Well, a future person did.

I excused myself in the middle of the job, saying Pratchett needed help with his long division homework, as if he weren't reading a high school algebra textbook for fun. Valhalla Hardware hadn't gone out of business yet, and that's where I bought ten L-shaped brackets. ("Corner braces," Mr. Jurgenson called them when he pointed me to the right drawer. "You fixing an old dresser or something?" I said that was exactly right.) Back home, I headed up the ladder with the braces and a screwdriver in my back pocket.

That's how I built a hidden ladder down from my bedroom window. *And* got paid to do it.

It came in handy many times, since the only other way out was what my family called the World's Noisiest Stairs.

Just after midnight on Tuesday, I slid my window open, feeling the rush of cool valley air spilling in. I eased one leg over the windowsill. Finding the first brace with my toe was harder than I remembered it being, probably because my pants were from sixth grade and were as tight as a leotard.

(Beef Squad rules were clear: If we were out late, everyone had to wear their LBJ concert blacks. We looked pretty silly sneaking around in chinos and polo shirts, but I couldn't argue with the results. The night of the textbook prank, we'd hidden in the shrubs alongside Busey Funeral Home while a police cruiser's spotlight doused the leaves. The cruiser rolled on. The concert blacks had worked—although Hogue claimed he had sent the cop away using the Force.)

Tight pants and all, I made it down the hidden rungs on the chimney, fetched my bike from the backyard, and rolled away as quietly as I could.

On the near side of the Esplanade Bridge, a path down to the water had been beaten over the years by the feet of Leonardville's kids. It led to a little strip of pebbles we called the Beach. We had caught our first bluegills at the Beach. When we floated down the creek from Chapin Mine, the Beach was where we stood up in the current, shouldered our inner tubes, and trudged back to civilization.

It was our mission rendezvous point.

As I bumped my wheels over the curb, I heard a loud "Pssst! Over here!"

That was Hogue's idea of being sneaky. At least the babble of the stream covered any noise we made.

I leaned my bike into a blackberry bush and headed down the path. The darkness didn't slow me; after all these years, I could walk the trail to the Beach with my eyes closed. It was a different place at night. The smells were richer. The distances seemed longer. When I ducked under the arch of wild grapevines and felt the gravel under my feet, I was in a secret realm.

In my entire life I had never once seen a grown-up on the Beach.

"Who all's here?" I asked Hogue before I could see him. My eyes hadn't adjusted to the deep shadows, and they never would. Because right then Hogue lit up his face with his phone's flashlight. I squinted my eyes shut as quick as my reflexes let me, but his goofy face—stretched wide into a terrifying silent scream—was seared onto the back of my eyeballs for the next half hour.

"Thanks for that, bruh," I said.

Pratchett came down a minute later, stepping through the vines and nodding to us wordlessly like a professional commando.

"Did you guys block Karla?" Hogue asked.

Pratchett and I said we did.

Earlier that day, Karla Woo had texted us, begging us not to attempt the mission. Jared immediately called us on group chat, insisting that we block her for the next twenty-four hours.

"She's gonna get in our heads, and that kind of doubt is poisonous," he said.

"I felt bad, but I did it, too," Hogue said in the darkness of the Beach.

Just then, a single word rang down from the bridge above. "Abort!"

"Jared, get down here," I hissed as loudly as I dared.

I heard his bike chain slap as he crossed the curb. Next I heard his panting. Then I heard his bike fall into a bush and a different sound—a hollow knocking, like bongo drums.

"Abort!" Jared repeated as he got close. "Abort, abort, abort. We gotta call it off."

He stepped down onto the Beach.

"What happened?" Pratchett said.

"Did the cops see you?" Hogue said.

Jared shook his head. "Check it," he said.

He turned away from us and bent forward. Apparently, I wasn't the only one growing out of his concert blacks. Because there, in the blackness of the creekside jungle, a white vertical stripe bloomed before our eyes.

Jared had split his pants.

It's a testament to our seriousness as covert operators that Hogue, Pratchett, and I stopped laughing in less than nine minutes. Okay, maybe twelve. Fifteen, tops.

"You guys enjoying this?" Jared said when we were finally able to stand up straight. "Sorry, but we gotta cut this laugh party short."

"I'm not sure torn pants are something we should abort over," Pratchett said.

"Oh, really," Jared said. "You want me to pull a mission with my butt showing?"

"Yes!" I said. "This is important for Mr. Easton. Besides, it's not your butt showing. It's just your underwear." I couldn't resist adding, "Your white, *white* underwear."

We descended into another bout of laughter.

"Laugh it up," Jared said. "But I'm out of here."

He turned to go, white underwear and all.

"Wait," Hogue said. "You can still finish the mission."

"Yeah, don't go," I said. "We'll stop laughing."

"We promise," Pratchett said.

"Promise?" Jared said.

"Yeah," Hogue said. "I think it actually makes you a better operator. It's like the stripe on a skunk. A warning to stay away."

"But you may have to fart to get the desired effect," I said.

Five minutes later—okay, seven, tops—the four of us climbed up from the creek.

Before we mounted our bikes, Jared showed us the source of the knocking sound: a large duffel containing the disassembled tubes, hoses, and tanks of Cold Vengeance.

"I figured it's better to have it and not need it than to need it and not have it," Jared said.

I didn't see how a water-balloon artillery piece would be useful for a job like this, but if it kept Jared and his ripped seams from going home, I wasn't going to argue.

Jared struggled getting the straps of the duffel over his shoulders. Pratchett guided his arms through the straps and then steadied his bike while he climbed on. He pushed off across the bridge and the rest of us scrambled to get our bikes and follow.

We turned off the Esplanade and closed the rest of the distance on side streets to make ourselves less obvious. The back lot at Butte Nuggets Hall was only big enough for a couple of parking spaces and a large dumpster. We were stashing our bikes behind the trash bin when Jared announced his plan.

"I'll set up over there," he said, pointing across the street to the Golden Bear Credit Union parking lot. "Maybe even across that next street, since I have the range."

"Wait, what?" I said.

"Cold Vengeance won't do much good inside," Jared said. "And you three are strong enough to carry one file of papers, I hope."

He handed me the notebook page containing our best guesses at the door codes, then started off on foot.

"What'll you do?" Pratchett said.

"Cover you," Jared said over his shoulder. "You know, if things get hot."

Tubes stuck up from his pack every which way. We watched him cross the street looking like a cartoon bagpiper.

The first combo I tried caused a faint buzzing sound and a click inside the wall. I pulled on the doorknob and the door swung open.

"Yes!" Hogue said.

In my excitement to get inside, I tried and failed to stuff

the notebook paper into my back pocket. It fluttered to the pavement. I stuck my toe into the doorway to keep the door from closing and bent down to pick up the paper.

That was when my pants split up the back with a sharp rending sound.

The next thing I heard was Jared's giddy voice from somewhere across the street.

"I heard that!"

CHAPTER 18

The three of us stood in a dim hallway. The only light came from an exit sign over our heads. I could smell the wood-paneled walls better than I could see them. As the door shut behind us, a draft of air fluttered the back of my pants.

"I hope your underwear is clean," Hogue said. "Because we have to look at it the rest of the night."

"No, you don't," I said. "It's totally dark in here."

"Not dark enough," Hogue said.

"Let's focus," Pratchett said, taking two printed pages from his pocket: maps he'd created on his tablet. He held them up to catch the exit sign's light. "The second story is the big meeting hall. The ground floor is smaller rooms, so this is probably where the offices are."

"Offices are *boring*," Hogue said.

"But that's where people keep files," I said.

"I guess it won't be as boring if we're stealing stuff," Hogue said.

Pratchett led the way to our left, pushing through a swinging door.

The darkness that surrounded us was so inky black I almost got dizzy. I was just about to turn on my phone's flashlight when suddenly every light in the room came on with a *thwack*. We were standing at one end of a large kitchen. Pans hung over the stove on one wall. A sink and a dishwasher took up the opposite wall. Cabinets and two industrial-size refrigerators took up the wall directly in front of us. Behind us, at the door where'd we come in, Hogue stood with his hand on the light switch.

"That's better, right?" Hogue said.

Pratchett said. "No lights!"

In our planning meeting in Jared's bedroom, we talked about how any light in the windows would attract attention. We would rely on flashlights only, and even those we would use sparingly. But Hogue didn't seem to remember or care.

"This place is cool!" Hogue said. "Maybe there's Popsicles in the fridge, like at school." Hogue started toward the refrigerators.

"Turn it off!" Pratchett hissed at me, pointing to the light switch.

"I think it's okay," I said. "There are no windows in here."

Pratchett looked around. "There are no files, either," he said. "Let's get going."

"Jackpot!" Hogue said, holding up a box of lime Popsicles. "You want one?"

"We have to keep moving!" Pratchett said. "This is a *mission*."

"Fine," Hogue said, crossing back our way with the box under his arm. "We'll have them after, as a reward."

Hogue flicked the light off as we exited back into the hall.

Pratchett headed to the next door, pulled it open, and shined his phone's light inside.

"Janitor closet," he said, pushing it shut.

The door after that was locked. Pratchett shined his light on the outside. A plaque was screwed into the wood. It said:

PAUL DEKKER
GRAND DONKEY

"Scott's dad is Grand Donkey!" Hogue said. "What's a Grand Donkey?"

"It's like a Grand Burro, but bigger," I said.

"Very funny, underwear boy," Hogue said.

"Actually," Pratchett said, "it means the president of the club. The Butte Nuggets started back when secret societies were popular. They gave their officers goofy names as a kind of inside joke. The town's mayor or a senator could be a Grand Donkey and no one outside the club would ever know."

"You mean grown-up clubs are just like Beef Squad?" Hogue said.

"Pretty much," Pratchett said.

"What are we waiting for?" Hogue said. "Kick in the door and let's get the file and get out of here."

"Dude, no!" Pratchett said. "We have to get the file without breaking anything. Then they'll just think they lost it, or maybe one of their own people took it. If Mr. Dekker finds his door busted, he's gonna call the cops."

"We can't pick locks," Hogue said. It was true. For all our skills at breaking through digital security systems, we were totally useless when it came to the century-old brass contraption in front of us.

That's when the texts from Jared started coming.

JARED
U guys get it?

ME
Not yet. Locked out of office.

JARED
LOL Loozers

Pratchett was on his knees trying to angle his phone camera through the crack beneath the door when Jared's next text came.

JARED
I found this for you loozers
[Video: "How to Pick a Skeleton-Key Lock."]

"Is this a skeleton-key lock?" I said.

"The old-timey kind with the big keyhole?" Pratchett said. "Looks like it."

The video was only three minutes long. The guy used two Allen wrenches, one to copy the lifting action of the skeleton key and the other to move the dead bolt.

"That's super easy!" Pratchett said. "We just need to find tools like that around here. Or something we can bend into that shape."

"Wait," I said. "How did Jared know it would be a skeleton key?"

"Because the building is a hundred and fifty years old," Pratchett said.

"For a dumb jerk, Jared's pretty smart," Hogue said. "Also nice, and not a jerk."

The hallway ended at a black curtain. Pratchett pushed that aside. We followed him through it and found ourselves in the building's lobby.

"Wow," I said.

Once again the exit signs gave just enough light. We could see the outlines of a chandelier hanging from the ceiling and the thick bannister rising with the stairway to the second-story balcony.

It was an unusual sight for us because, to put it kindly, Leonardville is not known for the fine ornamentation of our buildings. You could say our preferred architectural aesthetic is cement.

We followed Pratchett past the double doors on our right,

which were the same front doors we rode past on the Esplanade every school morning. (Until we got suspended, that is.) A heavy chain had been wrapped around the door handles and padlocked in the middle. I made a mental note that the back door was our only exit.

The wide staircase creaked horribly under our weight—almost as badly as the one in our house. I had to remind myself there was no one here to hear us. From the top of the stairs, there was just one way to go: through a wide double door that already stood partly open.

The meeting hall was almost pitch-black. We painted it with our flashlights, taking care not to raise them high enough to illuminate the half-circle windows. Towers of stacked chairs lined one wall. Beneath our feet, the carpet was so deep that for a second I thought I'd stepped in something.

The dark curtain of a stage yawned at the far end of the room, and that was where Pratchett headed.

"You look on that side," he said as he clomped up the stairs on the right-hand side of the stage. Hogue and I took the left. I found the edge of the curtain and held it open for Hogue and me.

On the other side we lit our phone flashlights without fear. The stage seemed to be set up for some kind of skit. The backdrop was painted—pretty well, I thought—to look like the foothills above Leonardville. An old-timey water well, complete with a bucket on a rope, sat in the middle of the stage. I shined my light into the well.

At the bottom were a green pillow and a photocopied script that said *The Beguiling Raccoon.*

"Why are grown-ups doing a play about raccoons?" Hogue said.

"That's a Butt Nugget secret you are not allowed to know," I said. It sounded like a joke, but I actually think it was true.

"A secret—awesome!" Hogue said.

He set the Popsicle box down, leaned all the way into the well, and grabbed the script.

That was when Hogue's pants split up the back.

"Nice tighty-whities, dude," I said.

"Thanks," Hogue said. He tried to play it off like he didn't care, but after he'd ridden me so hard about *my* underwear, I knew it had to sting.

"Are those your dad's?" I said, twisting the knife.

"What? Ew!" Hogue said. "That is foul, dude."

"Found something!" called Pratchett from the other side of the stage. He held up two knitting needles. "These were in a basket of props. We can bend them into right angles and they'll work just like the Allen wrenches in the video."

"Hogue ripped his pants," I said.

Pratchett blinked at me. Was he actually too excited at the prospect of picking Paul Dekker's lock to enjoy this moment?

"He's wearing tighty-whities," I added.

But Pratchett was already pulling the curtain aside to leave.

"See?" Hogue said. "*Your* underwear is funny. Mine isn't."

Pratchett used the gap under the office door as a brace to bend the needles. The video had made picking the lock look easy. But each time Pratchett had one knitting needle in place, the task of getting the second one into the right position always knocked the first one off its mark.

After about five minutes, Hogue said, "I *told* you we don't know how to pick locks."

Just then, the lock made a satisfying *thunk*.

"You were saying?" Pratchett said. He gave the knob a turn and the door swung inward.

The office of the Grand Donkey of the Butte Nuggets wasn't much. A metal desk faced the door, backed by some bookshelves. A frame on the wall showed a black-and-white photo of the hall from back in the days of horse-and-buggies.

"Let's find that file," Pratchett said, leafing through the papers on the desk. I went to a metal file cabinet under the photo while Hogue searched the bookshelves.

The drawer I rifled probably held more than a hundred files. These were some of the labels I read.

Pyrite Days Insurance

Mortgage Refi—2018

Past-Due Notices

X-Mas Party Rentals

Maldives House

Grand Donkey Elections (past)

Budget (Proposed by Ted)

Property Tax Bills

Letters of Rec.

Ladies' Aux. Budget

Carpet Cleaning

A bell rang in my memory, and I pulled the file that said "Maldives House." Inside were dozens of pages in a language I couldn't begin to decipher. The only things I could make out were a picture of a beach house and the name signed at the bottom of an official certificate: Paul Dekker.

That was as far as I got before another text came through to our phones. We all read it simultaneously:

JARED

Someone at back door, get out!!!

We barely had time to give each other stupid looks before we heard the back door slam. There was nowhere to run.

"Hide!" Pratchett whispered, diving under the desk. Hogue and I jumped on top of him.

The light flicked on.

"Get up, guys," said a familiar voice.

Under the desk, Pratchett, Hogue, and I shared a look of pure confusion. I got to my knees and looked over the desk.

Karla Woo stood there, leaning on the doorjamb. She wore denim shorts and a black hoodie over a pink T-shirt.

"What are *you* doing here?" I said.

"Attempting to save your stupid butts," she said. "It's a setup."

Through the ancient walls of Butte Nuggets Hall came the very modern sound of a police siren.

"But how did—" Pratchett started to ask.

"There's no time!" Karla said. "Come on!"

Hogue, Pratchett, and I untangled our legs and scrambled to our feet. I stuffed the file back and closed the cabinet, and we followed her out the office door. I probably ran down that hallway faster than I'd ever run before, but I might as well have taken my time. Because when we pushed through the back door, a police cruiser was already blocking the driveway. And leaning on the cruiser's hood was another familiar face from LBJ Middle School: Officer Jim.

Smiling, as usual.

CHAPTER 19

Blue and red lights flickered against the walls of the back lot, making the place look like a silent disco. My instincts told me to run back inside, but the door slammed closed behind us.

"It's okay, kids," Officer Jim said. "Everything's fine. I've got help on the way."

He said it so soothingly.

"Help for us?" Pratchett asked. Because that was what it sounded like.

But the answer arrived in the form of a second police cruiser. The doors swung open and two cops stood up, sliding their batons into rings on their belts.

"Hello, men," Officer Jim said to the two other cops without looking back. (He probably should have looked, since one of them was a woman.)

He told us to sit against the back wall of Butte Nuggets

Hall. Pratchett was the last to sit down. He was lowering himself into the space between Karla and me when his pants split up the back.

"Nice ones!" Hogue said, seeing Pratchett's printed boxer shorts. "Are those planets?"

Pratchett grumbled something about a souvenir from the planetarium in San Francisco.

Officer Jim spoke into the radio on his shoulder.

"Dispatch, I've got four juveniles in custody at the site of a ten-fourteen on Esplanade," he said. "Other units be advised: additional juvenile is likely at large in the vicinity, name of Jared Tamblyn."

"Run, Jared," Pratchett whispered. "Run!"

"Why *did* you come here?" Hogue whispered to Karla.

"I saw them texting about someone opening the back door of the hall," she said, "so I knew something weird was up. Luckily, I live three blocks away."

"You saw them *texting*?" I said.

"No talking!" the other policeman barked. The three officers were huddled in conversation just out of earshot.

Karla waited a respectful moment before continuing in a low voice.

"I broke the two-factor authentication for the alarm," she whispered.

Of course she did.

"So, two-factor meant you were already hacking their phones," Pratchett said. "And once you did that—"

"I could read their texts," she said.

No one talked for a minute as that sank in. Then a question dropped into my head.

"*Whose* texts?" I whispered.

"Paul Dekker," she said. Then she nodded toward the police cruiser. "And Officer Jim."

"*What?*" Pratchett hissed, but just then, Officer Jim and the other cops came our way.

The two partners crossed to the back door of the hall. The woman cop stepped to the keypad and consulted her phone.

"It's nine-three-nine-five," Hogue called to her.

She keyed the door open without acknowledging Hogue's help.

Another cruiser pulled up in the street. A single cop got out, holstering his baton like the others. He was older, with gray hair by his ears and stripes on his sleeve.

Suddenly Officer Jim's posture changed. He straightened up and used a hand to slick down his hair.

This cop was obviously the boss.

"You're out late," the older cop said to Officer Jim. "Alarm call?"

"Yessir," Officer Jim said. "I was in the area heading home for the night when the call went out about the back door being opened. My money would have been on rats chewing the wire, but instead I found these creatures."

He lifted an arm toward us.

The back door opened and the other two police officers came out. They greeted their boss and handed some items to Officer Jim: the bent knitting needles. Officer Jim made a show of inspecting them thoroughly. He tested their points with the tip of a finger.

"Any vandalism?" the boss cop asked the partners.

"None we could find," the woman cop said.

"Any stolen goods?" he said.

"I haven't searched them yet," Officer Jim said.

"Well, that shouldn't take long," the boss said.

He came our way. His name tag said SGT. JORDAN.

"All right, kids, stand up," he said.

We did as he said.

"Hold your arms out like this," he said.

We followed his example and made a T with our arms.

"Now turn around," he said.

We did.

"Holy macaroni!" Sergeant Jordan said. "What happened to y'all's pants?"

In my peripheral vision I saw Officer Jim approach Hogue, but I couldn't tell what he did.

"Permission to turn around, sir," Pratchett said.

"Go ahead," Sergeant Jordan said. "All you."

I gratefully rotated my butt back to the wall.

"Our pants are all from sixth grade," Pratchett said. "So they're way too tight."

"Well, I'd ask why you're wearing tight pants," the sergeant said, "but my bigger question is why'd you break into the Butte Nuggets Hall?"

"We didn't break in," I said. "We *let* ourselves in."

"Okay, but why?" the sergeant said. "What are you after?"

"We were curious," Pratchett said.

"Yeah," Hogue said. "We wanted to see what the big deal was with a secret grown-up club."

"And what did you find out?" Sergeant Jordan said.

"It's just like a kids' club," Hogue said. "But with a fancier building."

"Sounds about right," the sergeant said, nodding. "I search your pockets, am I going to find anything?"

We shook our heads.

"No so fast," Officer Jim said. "This was in that one's back pocket," he said, pointing at Hogue. He handed Sergeant Jordan a bundle of photocopied papers.

Sergeant Jordan held the papers out with one hand while retrieving his flashlight from his belt with the other. He flicked the light on and read the first page.

" 'The Beguiling Raccoon'?" he said. He looked to Officer Jim for an explanation.

"A dramatic script," Officer Jim said. "Property of the Butte Nuggets, for use in a private ceremony of some sort." He held up the bent knitting needles. "Additionally, I'm willing to bet these knitting needles were bent by these kids. That makes illegal entry for purposes of theft or mayhem."

The sergeant let out a loud sigh.

"Officer Jim, are you suggesting that we *book* these kids?" he asked with wide eyes. "Instead of just calling their parents like we always do? Have they got any prior arrests?"

"No," Officer Jim said. "Look, I'm not happy about it, but I happen to be on good terms with the Butte Nuggets leadership, and I'm certain they would want to press charges."

"Oh! Is that what this is about?" Sergeant Jordan said. "You trying to get in good with the Nuggets, Officer Jim?"

"No, I just think—" Officer Jim said, but his superior officer cut him off.

"I've heard what you *think,* patrolman, and I am not impressed," Sergeant Jordan said. "Reminds me of the time you dusted for fingerprints in the refrigerator to find out who was taking your yogurt."

The other two cops tried to smother their laughter.

"Now," the sergeant said, "maybe you want to stay up all night typing reports about knitting needles, but I most certainly do not want to read them. And I darn sure don't want this to be the kind of police force that jails a coupla kids."

"Yessir," Officer Jim said.

"You got your cell phone?" the sergeant said.

"Yessir," Officer Jim said, pulling it from his belt.

"How many bars you got?" Sergeant Jordan said.

"All of them," Officer Jim said.

"Hallelujah!" Sergeant Jordan said. "Whatchou gonna do with it?"

"Call their parents," Officer Jim said. He seemed unable to look his boss in the eye.

"And then what?" Sergeant Jordan said.

"Wait for them to show up," Officer Jim said.

"Uh-huh?" Sergeant Jordan said.

"Then go home and go to sleep," Officer Jim said.

"And?" Sergeant Jordan said.

"And that's an order?" Officer Jim said.

"Exactly," the sergeant said. He straightened his hat, turned, and walked toward his car.

He had almost made it when the water balloon burst on top of his head.

CHAPTER 20

Hogue and I rode in Officer Jim's car. Karla and Pratchett rode with the woman cop and her partner. Jared rode alone with the soaking-wet Sergeant Jordan.

The water-balloon attack had lasted nearly a minute, involving seventeen balloons that had fallen with surprising accuracy. Jared later claimed he had been aiming for Sergeant Jordan's head, which was hard to believe. But in addition to drenching the ranking officer on the scene, Jared scored a direct hit on one of the other patrol cops, splattered pretty much all of us to the point that our clothes stuck to our skin, rinsed all three police cruisers with loud impacts on their roofs and hoods, and sent a one-in-a-million shot through Officer Jim's driver's-side window.

When it was over, Jared bellowed from across the parking lot, "Run, you idiots! Run! Run now!"

Jared was easily caught by the woman cop. She walked across the lot and grabbed his shirt collar before he could wriggle his arms through the duffel straps.

What choice did Sergeant Jordan have except to book us all into jail? "You're lucky we're sparing the handcuffs on your ungrateful butts," Sergeant Jordan said as we got into the cars. In fact, I *was* grateful not to be handcuffed, but I knew better than to tell him that.

The officers loaded our bikes into their cruiser trunks. The handlebars hung out like the antlers of four unfortunate beasts.

Viewed from the street, the Leonardville Police Department headquarters is a sleekly modern public building. Weeping willows drape over the front, illuminated by lights set down into the earth. It all adds up to a welcoming mood.

That's the side of the building they want you to see. Officer Jim pulled around back, which is darker and more industrial. A loading dock for criminals.

Which was exactly what we were.

"Crazy kids," the sergeant muttered as the nine of us walked from the parking lot to the station. "What I get for trying to help your sorry torn butts? Water up in every darn thing."

He left to go change. Feeling the breeze on the back of my thighs, I wished I could change, too. That wouldn't happen for a long time.

Officer Jim held a steel door open for us. When we were

all through, he led us up a hall to a woman in a blue sweater who sat behind a counter. It was a kiosk like you see at the bank.

"Waddawe got here?" she said.

"Conspiracy, breaking and entering," Officer Jim began, "weapons and explosives charges, burglary—"

"Wait!" I said. "We didn't steal anything!"

"If I was using explosives, you would have known it," Jared said.

Officer Jim didn't even look back at us.

"Let's get the booking docs worked up and go from there."

A lot of the details of getting arrested are super boring, so I'll just say I never expected to have my fingerprints scanned into an FBI database before I graduated from middle school.

For a few minutes, Officer Jim left the five of us sitting together on a hard bench. It was the first chance we'd all had to talk since before everything went down.

"Man, we were almost home free," I said to Jared. "Then you went full D-Day on us."

"That was the plan!" Jared said.

"It was *your* plan," Pratchett said.

"No," Jared said. "My plan was to warn you to get away, which I did."

"Actually," Pratchett said, "Karla's the one who warned us."

"What?" Jared said.

Karla nodded to him.

"She broke their two-factor, too," Pratchett said.

"That is total bull!" Jared said. But his curiosity overtook his pride. "Wait, really?"

Karla nodded again, her face as blank as the police station walls.

Officer Jim reentered the waiting area.

"Ms. Woo, please come with me."

The interrogations began. Karla went with him, and we didn't see her again that night. About a half hour later it was Pratchett's turn, and a while after that, Officer Jim called for me.

He took me to a little room just like the one on the cop show my parents watch. There was a wide mirror built into the wall, which I knew was see-through from the other side. A video camera blinked on a tripod in the corner. An eye screw was bolted into the table for when they handcuffed someone there.

"Mr. Rhodes," Officer Jim said in a cheery tone. "Take a seat, chief."

His mood seemed to have recovered after the sergeant's humiliation. He must have been pretty pleased that the water balloon assault had bypassed the "just call their parents" route.

He said both our names and the date, then read me my rights. When he was done, he asked me if I understood them. I nodded.

"Can you say it out loud?" Officer Jim said.

"Yes, I understand," I said.

"Okay, great," Officer Jim said. "Your two friends were helpful. Hopefully you'll be helpful, too. Let's start with the basics, and then we'll get to the fun stuff. What were you doing in the vicinity of Butte Nuggets Hall tonight?"

I shrugged.

"Again, can you say it out loud?" he said.

I shook my head. I had heard the sergeant tell Officer Jim that they didn't have much evidence against us. The last thing I was going to do was give him more.

"Come on, you're a smart kid," he said. "This is your chance to help yourself. Tell me what you were up to."

I raised my eyebrows microscopically higher. The cops on TV used this "help yourself" strategy all the time.

"Look, I get it," Officer Jim said, leaning closer over the table. "I understand you have been led astray. So let's talk about that. It can't be just a coincidence that every member of the LBJ robotics team got arrested tonight. Can it?"

He had my attention, and he knew it.

"That's right," he said. "All five of you, out after midnight, breaking and entering, vandalism and mayhem against a civic club, *and* assaulting the police using a piece of sophisticated engineering that an adult must have helped you build."

"What are you saying?" I asked.

"I'm saying that all this can go away," he said, waving a hand around to indicate the police station. "No breaking-

and-entering charges, no theft or vandalism charges, no explosives or terrorism charges—"

"Terrorism?" I said. "Are you *kidding*?"

"All of it goes away and you go home a free man tonight," Officer Jim said. "If you just tell me the truth about the man who made you a criminal."

"You mean—" I stopped short.

I finally realized what he was asking me to say. I eyed the video camera.

"Yes!" Officer Jim said, pointing at the camera. "Look into the camera and say his name! Think about your warm, warm bed, Nick! You could be there in twenty minutes. All I want is two words, and you know what they are, because they're the truth! Isn't that right?"

Officer Jim was practically crawling across the table toward me. I had never seen him like this before.

"I want that name, Nick!" he said. "This isn't your fault, and you know it! You're a straight-A student! You're a good kid, and this is all someone else's doing! Now give me his name!"

"You mean—"

"Yes, Nick?" Officer Jim said. "Say the magic words, Nick Rhodes! Say the words that will set you free!"

"Mr. Easton?"

CHAPTER

21

So right around now you're probably saying, "Super-cool story, Nick. Can we talk about this whole 'Beef Squad' name thing?"

Okay. The origin of our name is nothing exciting. We've never ridden on a cattle drive to Dodge City. We've never wrapped our fists in tape and punched frozen steers in preparation for a title boxing match. Beef isn't even our favorite food—Pratchett's actually a vegetarian.

Like all of our best stories, it started with a video game.

There was an indie game from Japan that Hogue insisted we play because he was a fan of the art director's manga.

"If you don't love *Sneaker Samurai,* don't ever talk to me again," he said as we first logged on.

We didn't love it. In fact, it was a total snooze. We each played a shoe: a little white, green, or yellow sneaker with dangling laces. Our job was to hopscotch on the correct squares to collect the points written there in chalk. Every time we collected a big number our shoes made this noise like a goose honking and a little egg would pop out of the sneaker and float up to our "nest" in the corner of the screen.

You know, pretty much your standard hopping-shoe-that-lays-goose-eggs game. If we landed on one of the dog-poop squares, the eggs all cracked and our score zeroed out in a brown splash.

And people thought stupidball had weird rules.

Twenty hours later, even Hogue had changed his position: "If you like this game, don't ever talk to me again."

Sneaker Samurai did give us a shared joke that lived on long after we had deleted it from our PCs. Before each level, the team of shoes got a briefing from their commanding officer—a basketball shoe named General Hightop. But the translation from Japanese was off. Instead of saying "Squad briefing," General Hightop said "Brief squad." And since everything about the game was janky, it sounded like "Beef Squad."

It became our own private meme, an all-purpose phrase. We used it to mean anything from "Hello" to "Thank you" to "Do you have the pre-algebra homework, cuz I left my backpack in Dad's car and he went to play racquetball with Gary."

Within a few days, we were calling ourselves Beef Squad. Within a couple more, other people were, too.

Part of me hopes everyone knows that *we* know it's dumb. But another part of me couldn't care less.

We're Beef Squad. Deal with it.

I tell the story now because there's a lesson in it: you never know how a few words will come to define you.

After that night, we were defined by two new words: "Mr. Easton."

All of us had said his name out loud. And even though we'd protested and sworn he wasn't involved, the damage was done.

It was just what his enemies wanted. The school board had apparently been itching to fire Mr. Easton over the firecrackers lesson and whatever other lines he'd crossed over the years. But firing a teacher isn't easy. They needed more, and we gave it to them.

After we got home from the police station, none of us could sleep, so we started texting.

JARED
If code was correct, how did they know we were there?

KARLA
Dekker had alert 4 any time door opened. I just found it now

PRATCHETT
He couldn't monitor 24 hrs/day. Had to know we were commode

PRATCHETT
+Coming

HOGUE

I am commode!

ME

Autocorrect FTW, Prat. So Mr. Dekker knew Scott told
me about file. Maybe Scott confessed to him?

JARED

That would mean Scott felt bad 1st time + told you,
then felt bad anOthEr time + told HIM he told you. That
weasel never felt bad about nothing

ME

Then why did he tell me about evidence to begin w?

PRATCHETT

I don't think there was any evidence

KARLA

WE ARE THE EVIDENCE

HOGUE

I am evidence and commode!

We risked it all to save Mr. Easton from getting fired only
to end up being the thing that would *get* him fired. It felt
terrible.

Of course, we had plenty of our own troubles to worry

about. Starting with the people who drove us home from the police station at four in the morning: our parents.

We were all grounded until further notice, obviously. No video games for the rest of time, no discussion.

When my interrogation with Officer Jim finally ended and I walked out to the front of the police station, the sight of my parents sitting on a bench under a Neighborhood Watch poster was both comforting and horrible. I was *so* relieved to be going home, to my own bed, with people who loved me. But I knew how upset they had to be. Especially Mom, who had recently convinced herself I was back on a path toward righteousness.

I didn't know what to say to them other than sorry.

Wednesday was supposed to be our big return to school. Believe me, *that* was one rough morning. I don't know if it was the lack of sleep or the breaking of my parents' hearts—probably both—but our breakfast table was so quiet I could hear all three of us chewing at the same time.

I was packing my lunch when the phone rang.

"Hi, Brent," my dad said after picking up. Brent being the first name of Vice Principal Brent Michael Hopper. "It was a long night, thanks. . . . Thanks . . . Thanks . . . Thanks . . . I understand, Brent. Thanks."

He hung up.

My mom looked up from her oatmeal.

"Nick's not welcome back at school today," my dad said.

My mom looked down at her oatmeal.

"Brent wants to have a parent conference this afternoon," he said.

My mom took a sip of her coffee and put her mug back down to speak her only words of the morning: "Why did you keep telling him 'Thanks'?"

The conference wasn't just for me; it was for all five of us and our parents. Vice Principal Hopper had reserved the library, since his office wouldn't hold fifteen people. Seeing all our parents—best friends—greet each other with such grim recognition put a bitter taste in my mouth. They were always so jokey. *Way too* jokey, in fact!

Now it was like someone had died. What I wouldn't have given for a lame pun.

Karla Woo's parents sat in the back corner of the back row of seats, with Karla between them. When I caught her eye, she just raised her eyebrows. That could have meant anything.

When we were all seated, Officer Jim entered like he was walking onto a talk-show stage: all smiles, shaking the hands of the few parents who offered them. Somehow he was the only one who looked like he'd gotten a full night's sleep.

Even Vice Principal Hopper's eyes were bloodshot. I wondered if someone had woken him up with the news of our arrest.

"Okay, let's start talking," Vice Principal Hopper said, standing in front of the little audience.

"Can we talk about asparagus?" Hogue said. His mom patted his leg.

Vice Principal Hopper kept right on going.

"I've been informed by Officer Jim about last night's incident at Butte Nuggets Hall," he said. "It's a matter we have to take very seriously."

Jared raised his hand but didn't wait to be called.

"Even though it was a total setup?" he said.

"We're still finding out what happened," Vice Principal Hopper said.

"What happened is we were set up," Pratchett said.

"Total setup," Hogue said.

Vice Principal Hopper sighed.

"Officer Jim, would you like to explain the chain of events?" he said.

"Happy to," Officer Jim said, standing from his chair. "Sometime between zero-one-hundred and zero-one-thirty, a door alarm from Butte Nuggets Hall sent a signal to the Leonardville Police Department—"

"Not true," Pratchett said.

But Officer Jim kept going.

"I was coming off a shift and happened to be the nearest unit, so I responded, and found your kids at the crime scene. During questioning on the scene, four members of the Leonardville PD were assaulted by improvised firearms—"

"Water balloons," I said, but again he ignored the interruption.

"—and the decision was made to take all five juveniles into custody," he said. "Which we did. And you all know the rest."

"You couldn't have gotten a door alarm, because we *disabled* the door alarm," Jared said.

"Son, I don't think that sounds as good as you think it sounds," Jared's dad said.

"Oh yeah?" Jared said. Then he leveled a finger at Officer Jim. "Well, *he's* a crooked cop!"

"Hey, now!" Officer Jim said.

"This is all off the record, right?" Jared's dad asked Vice Principal Hopper. "There's a lot of high emotion here." He gave Officer Jim an apologetic wave.

"It's not emotion," Pratchett said. "It's the truth."

"There is absolutely no truth to that," Officer Jim said flatly.

"Oh, yeah?" Karla Woo suddenly said. "Why don't you tell them who texted you? Do you think we don't know?"

"And while you're at it," Hogue said, "tell them about the perfectly good Popsicles you let melt!"

"Hey, hey, hey!" Vice Principal Hopper said. I saw panic in his eyes. "Let's talk about the facts at hand."

"The fact is this is bogus!" I said.

"Yeah!" Jared said.

"A complete setup and a sham," Pratchett said.

Vice Principal Hopper had lost control of the room. Who knows what would have happened if my mother hadn't stood up. Just the sight of her, a towering five foot four in heels, quieted our rebellion and caused everybody, kids and grown-ups alike, to wait for whatever she would say.

"Every week at the law firm, I hear people saying crooked cops set them up," she said. "Sometimes we even tell those stories in court, hoping a jury will buy that some big conspiracy is really to blame for all this guy's trouble. You know what all those people have in common?" She cast a glance at me. "They're guilty. So please, Mr. Hopper, cut to the chase and tell us the punishment. I'm sure it'll be fair. I think I speak for all the families here when I say we'll accept it and move on."

The other parents murmured their agreement.

"Fine," Vice Principal Hopper said. "Your children are all expelled."

My mother screamed, "Over my dead body, you crooked goon!"

CHAPTER
22

My mom once called True North Academy for Excellence "half school, half cult, and half factory."

"That's three halves," I said.

"I guess they're not too good at math, either," she said as we drove past the academy's converted warehouse.

Naturally, I was surprised when my parents announced that I would be going there. It was after dinner the same day we were expelled.

"What about the others?" was my first question.

They shared an uneasy look.

"They're going, too," my dad said. "But we want this to be a fresh start. For *you*."

I didn't like the sound of that, so I didn't ask what he meant. As usual, Mom told me anyway.

"We don't want you hanging out with them anymore," she said.

My stomach sank. My ears started ringing.

"Why not?" I asked.

"Mostly because of the sneaking-out-and-getting-arrested thing," my mom said. "That's kind of a deal-breaker in this house. Other houses, too! All the parents agree."

"That wasn't our fault!" I said.

"Oh, I guess Officer Jim forced you to make a hidden ladder on side of the chimney," Mom said.

I must have looked just as surprised as I felt.

"Yes, we found it," Mom said. "It wasn't hard."

"We knew you didn't sneak down the World's Noisiest Stairs," Dad said. "This is a second chance for you, and you're lucky to get it. Do you know they're talking about charging you guys with assaulting a police officer?"

Reflexively, I started to defend myself.

"But—"

What could I say that would make a difference? They were right. My friends and I had gotten arrested and expelled from school. Even worse, Officer Jim hadn't followed through on the "no charges" part of his deal. Maybe Jared calling him crooked in front of all those people had caused him to reconsider. In any case, one of the lawyers Mom knew had called that night to say the district attorney was still deciding what to do with us.

"Get some sleep," Mom said. "This place starts early."

I could still see my breath the next morning when I climbed into my mom's passenger seat, bringing along a backpack that contained nothing but a sack lunch.

"Next week you can start riding your bike," she said as I buckled the seat belt. "Because I think I'm still dreaming."

Cruising through the gray streets, I felt awful, both from waking up at five-thirty and from the terror of starting a new school. How would I fit in at this barn by the train tracks? My mom pulled into the True North drop-off lane, which was much shorter than the one at LBJ. As she neared the front, my anxiety worsened. My only comfort came from knowing that my friends would be there, too.

You know, the friends I was no longer allowed to hang out with.

The car ahead of us pulled away and Mom rolled up to the drop point.

"Don't get expelled again," my mom said, leaning over to give me a hug. "Believe me, you do not want me to home-school you. Now go. I love you very much."

A young man I assumed was a teacher opened my door for me. The air pimpled my arms as I stood up. The teacher shut the car's door and extended his hand. He wore a blue polo shirt embroidered with a seven-pointed star on the breast.

"Welcome, Scholar!" he said as we shook.

I found out quickly that True North Academy of Excellence had no kids, students, children, or pupils. We were all "Scholars."

With a capital "S."

"Thanks," I said.

Over his shoulder I noticed a line of kids in similar shirts. They were filing onto a yellow school bus, I guessed for a field trip. But something was off. Normally, kids leaving school behave like animals sprung from cages. These kids were quiet. They didn't jostle each other or take cuts in line. It was like they'd been on this field trip a hundred times.

I called it a converted warehouse, but there really wasn't much in the way of conversion. The double glass doors leading into the front office were obviously as old as the building. One of panes had a spiderweb crack.

"Welcome, Scholar!" the secretary said when I entered and introduced myself. "Head Smith is waiting for you."

Somebody's first name was Head?

"How do you do, Scholar?" Head Smith said when I went through her open office door. (It turned out "head" was what they called her instead of "principal.") Pratchett, Hogue, Jared, and Karla were already there, two seated and two standing up. "I'm so pleased you Scholars are joining our movement," Head Smith said, closing the door.

She wore a suit so dark I couldn't decide if it was blue or black. Her hair came down in a smooth, almost solid surface to her shoulders, where it flipped upward again. It looked like a hairdo designed to deflect falling objects back into the sky.

Her office could not have been more different from Vice Principal Hopper's. The walls rose to a normal height but then stopped. The warehouse ceiling was still another ten feet up, so the sounds of kids and teachers beginning their day echoed down on us. More than that, there were no photos, no plaques, no signs of her private life away from school. There wasn't even a window. One wall had been painted with the school's seven-star logo. The other walls had three standard motivational posters: the one with the kitten hanging from a branch, the one with the three seagulls gliding past the sunset, and the one with the bear snatching a fish out of midair.

"Now, I know all about you Scholars and your time at LBJ," she said in a warm tone. "I know you Scholars were the rejects, the failures, the outcasts, the people no one wanted."

"Actually—" Pratchett said, but she kept going.

"I have a different opinion of you Scholars," Head Smith said. "I look at you and I don't see misshapen, poorly performing, subintelligent roustabout losers."

"That's a relief," Hogue said.

"I see diamonds in the rough!" Head Smith said. "Maybe you were incapable of being successful students in a *school*."

"Um, we all got straight—" Karla started to say before Head Smith cut her off.

"You are certainly capable of being successful Scholars in a community! That's what True North Academy for Excellence is: a community! All you need is one thing. Do you know what that one thing is?"

"To believe in ourselves?" I said. It seemed like a can't-miss answer.

"Nope," Head Smith said. "A blue polo shirt."

She reached into a desk drawer and took out five shirts wrapped in clear plastic. She handed them to Karla to pass out.

"Once you wear the True North star on your breast, there's no going back," she said confidently.

Jared took his shirt and repeated a line his father had used on him the afternoon before.

"I don't think that sounds as good as you think it does."

As we were filing out of her office, Head Smith took a lighter and a bundle of sticks from her drawer. She lit the ends of the sticks on fire, then blew them out, waving the smoldering twigs through the air above her desk.

"What are you doing?" Hogue said.

"Purifying the air with mugwort," Head Smith said. Great, the principal of this "movement" was a witch.

The classrooms were built out of the same half-walls that made Head Smith's office. But that was the least bizarre thing about the place.

In Numbers 1, which was the math class, every student had a calculator out on their desk. Jared and I received them as soon as we sat down. But the lesson was less about math than it was about the function of the DallasTech Model 1501-G. Mr. Ahmet read aloud straight from the tiny directions booklet. Don't get me wrong—the thing's pretty cool. It was way more fun than solving problems on paper. Still, I had to wonder how well Numbers 1 was preparing us for high school math. Or any real-life situation without a fancy robot calculator.

Words 1 (you guessed it—that was English class) was even weirder. The teacher, Ms. Yarnell, handed Hogue and me copies of the book the class was reading. I looked at the cover and raised my hand.

"I got the wrong book," I said.

"Uh-oh," Ms. Yarnell said. "What do you have there?"

"The user manual to the PhotoMagic Enigma Series M9 Printer-Scanner-Photocopier," I said.

"No, that's right," Ms. Yarnell said.

Hogue lifted his book to show me he'd received the same thing.

"We're reading technical texts this quinmester," Ms. Yarnell said. "Why is that?"

She searched the class for a raised hand. She got one from a girl with two ponytails sticking out above her ears.

"Yes, Scholar," Ms. Yarnell said.

"Because technology is the biggest story of all," she said.

"And?" Ms. Yarnell said.

"And the Scholars of True North Academy for Excellence are going to be the heroes of that story," the ponytailed Scholar said.

We spent the next ninety minutes taking turns reading aloud about two-sided printing, replacing toner cartridges, and how to fix a paper jam without damaging the drums or belts.

"Okay, so—kind of weird," Pratchett admitted at lunch.

"Kind of?" Karla said.

"Okay, supremely weird," Pratchett said.

"That should be the school motto," I said.

The five of us sat together at a picnic table in the former loading dock. The view across the railroad spur was not inspiring, but it beat sitting inside, where three hundred people under one roof with no real walls made a noise that I can't describe.

Karla chuckled ruefully.

"What?" I said.

"I thought the day I started at LBJ was the worst day of my life," she said. "Nothing could top it. Now I've been arrested, expelled, and sent someplace even worse. I am *so* furious at you guys."

"So why are you eating lunch with us?" Jared said.

"You think I'm taking my chances with anyone in *there*?" Karla said. "I have no choice but to be friends with you!"

"Hi, friend!" Hogue said, extending his hand.

Karla sighed heavily and shook it.

"If I get called 'Scholar' one more time I'm going to throw this shirt in the three-cycling bin," Jared said.

Just then, a teacher came around the corner.

"Aha! There you are, Scholars," he said.

"That's it," Jared said, yanking the shirt up to his armpits. If Hogue hadn't grabbed his hands, I think he really would have done it.

"Cooling off outside, I see," the teacher said.

"Yeah," I said. "We're used to eating our lunch half naked."

"I see!" the teacher said. I recognized him as the one who

had greeted me at drop-off. He had googly eyes that didn't always point in the same direction. "Well, I'm Mr. Grindle. I teach the Advanced Scholars, and I wanted to talk about the experiences you bring to True North. I've been asking around, and it sounds like you Scholars have some proficiency with technology?"

None of us said anything for a few seconds. Across the tracks, a leaf blower started up.

"We're the LBJ robotics team," Karla said at last. "Well, we *were.*"

"Really, it was just her," Hogue said. "The rest of us played video games."

"That's so wonderful!" Mr. Grindle said. "True North is actually involved in an initiative for Advanced Scholars to apply high-tech solutions to real-world problems in real time, on a going-forward basis, with best practices *and* full redundancy. Does that sound like something you Scholars might like?"

Somewhere across the tracks a dog barked.

"It sounds like *something,*" Hogue finally said.

"Excellent!" Mr. Grindle said, clapping three times. "Because I've already signed you up for tomorrow's shift. Don't be late! The bus leaves the parking lot at six-forty-five sharp."

He walked back the way he'd come, quietly clapping his hands.

I thought about mentioning the line of kids I'd seen

getting on the bus that morning, but I kept quiet. They'd find out soon enough.

"You know why I think they call us all 'Scholar'?" Hogue said. "So they don't have to learn our names."

Jared said, "I think Scholar, here, is right."

CHAPTER

23

"Look at these wonderful new Scholars on Remote Team!" Mr. Grindle said at 6:45 the next morning, standing at the front of the bus.

A round of quiet applause came from behind us, where the rest of Remote Team sat.

I turned and waved, which earned me a swat on my thigh from Jared.

"What?" I whispered.

"This might be a murder bus," he said in my ear.

Jared was nervous because Mr. Grindle had taken all our phones before we got on the bus. I have to admit it was a total murderer move.

"These will stay here so everyone can keep themselves focused," he said, passing the bucket of phones to a Scholar who remained behind.

We didn't get murdered. Instead we got driven along the

eastern edge of town, past the last of the houses, past the golf course, which was still covered in a zillion silvery dewdrops. I remembered the time we'd fished in the lake there and Jared caught a largemouth bass the size of a football before we got chased off by a guy in a cook's apron.

The bus turned left onto a new road, which cut across a field of electric-green wild oats. In another month they would dry into golden foxtails that would stick in our socks all summer. If we wore socks. But for now they swayed gently in the morning breeze, daring anyone to run through.

I leaned into the aisle to see what lay ahead. A modern building stood in the middle of the field, looking as natural as a toaster in a flower bed. The bus slowed and we turned into the parking lot. The driver nosed the bus alongside a skimpy tree, killed the engine, and levered the bus doors open.

"Okay, Scholars, let's do some good today!" Mr. Grindle said.

We followed Mr. Grindle onto the pavement. I noticed a little cloth sack hanging from his belt. We walked in a ragged line toward the building, which I could now see was the government headquarters for Rust County. (Rust County was named after the red earth in the nearby hills. But it didn't take much imagination to see it as a comment on the general state of things in our corner of the world.)

I noticed another blue-shirted Scholar coming up from behind me. He looked older, high-school aged, with wavy blond hair combed way over to one side.

"What's the deal here?" I said to him. "What does Remote Team do?"

"Don't you know?" he said without looking at me. "Remote Team applies high-tech solutions to real-world problems in real time, on a going-forward basis, with best practices and full redundancy."

"I love redundancy," Hogue said, walking on my other side. "It's so—what's the word?"

"Redundant?" Pratchett said.

"Exactly!" Hogue said.

Mr. Grindle led us into a shallow lobby, then straight on to the elevators. I was looking forward to the ride up, since Leonardville only has three elevators, and one of them is in the hospital. Instead of pressing the button to give us a lift, Mr. Grindle yanked open the door to the stairs.

The stairs *down.*

"Huh," Jared said suspiciously.

A hundred sneakers squeaked on the painted concrete steps before we stepped through a heavy door. The hallway carpet was gray, with regularly spaced pools of light from overhead.

We walked toward another heavy door marked RECORDS.

"Cool!" Hogue said. "My dad collects records."

"I don't think it's that kind of records," I said.

Smaller than a gymnasium but much larger than any classroom, the chamber had a low ceiling full of fluorescent lights. No windows, shelves, or pictures interrupted the long walls, which were painted the color of Granny Smith apples.

The records—books and boxes of files from over a hundred years of county business—sat in overstuffed bookshelves to our right, and by the looks of it, more of them had once taken up the entire space.

But not anymore.

Almost half the floor was occupied by the instruments of Remote Team's high-tech solution: dozens of identical machines. I recognized them at once. So did Jared, who let out a low whistle.

"The PhotoMagic Enigma Series M9 Printer-Scanner-Photocopier," he said.

"No wonder we're all studying how to use it," Karla said.

"There must be thirty of them," I said.

"He wasn't kidding about redundancy," Pratchett said.

Mr. Grindle took the cloth sack from his belt. The members of Remote Team filed past him, each taking a thumb drive from the sack, then fanned out toward their work stations. But they seemed in no hurry to actually reach them.

"Excuse me," Hogue said, raising a hand toward the fluorescent tubes.

"Yes, Scholar," Mr. Grindle said. "Aren't they beautiful?" He swept an arm toward the rows of machines.

"Can I go back to school?" Hogue said. "This looks super boring."

Mr. Grindle cocked his head to one side. "There seems to be a misunderstanding," he said.

Hogue repeated himself, adding broad gestures to make himself clear.

"This . . . ," he said, jerking his thumb toward the printer-scanner-copiers, "looks . . . ," he said, pointing to his eyeballs for emphasis, "super . . ." Now he raised a fist in the air like the Man of Steel in mid-flight. "BORING!" he said, tapping his mouth with his hand like he was covering a yawn.

"No, I understood *you* perfectly," Mr. Grindle said, laughing nervously. "It's *you* who doesn't understand. See, Remote Team is a *privilege*."

"Where we're from, a privilege is, like, watching a movie in class," Jared said.

"Yeah, or playing dodgeball," I said.

Mr. Grindle laughed again, nodding.

"That's just it," he said. "We all know where you came from and what happened there. So, you can *say* you don't want to help Remote Team do this important work, but—"

Hogue tried to interrupt.

"I don't want to help Remote Team do this impo—"

"But," Mr. Grindle continued, "if you showed a little teamwork? I would really appreciate it. Okay? Okay. Great. Thanks."

It sank in what he was saying. We were criminals, so we had to work in this basement.

Remote Team's high-tech solution was to use the Photo-Magic Enigma Series M9s to scan records from Rust County's archives into digital files. Birth certificates, death certificates, land ownership documents—everything that remained in the rows of shelving on the other half of the room.

The newer documents were loose papers filed in cardboard boxes. The older ones were leather-bound books, with entries handwritten on the pages. The books gave the room the smell of a library.

As noobs—or "Rising Scholars," in Mr. Grindle's vocabulary—our job was to haul. We hauled documents from the stacks to any Scholar who was running low at their PhotoMagic Enigma Series M9. Then we hauled the scanned papers to "the dump," which is what they called the row of four bins in the corner. Every hour or so we'd wheel the bins to a space next to the freight elevator, then tip the contents into a large dumpster.

The pace was steady enough that I was sweating in just a few minutes.

After about an hour, Mr. Grindle announced he was going upstairs to find cell reception but would be back soon.

I collected a couple heavy volumes of land records from the Scholar with the wavy blond hair combed to one side.

"This doesn't seem too educational," I said.

"It's a real-world solution delivered in real time—" he began.

"I know, I know, with best practices and full redundancy," I said. "But after about fifteen minutes, we've learned all the best practices, right?"

For the first time, the Scholar looked at me.

"Learn?" he said. "Remote Team isn't about *learning*."

He shouted to the room, "Hey! This Rising Scholar thought we were here to *learn*!"

For a few seconds, the basement cavern was filled with a sound I hadn't heard since we came to True North Academy for Excellence: laughter.

Lunch was tuna-fish sandwiches on white buns from the county cafeteria. We ate sitting on the floor around the machines.

"Who wants to lead us today?" Mr. Grindle said while we ate.

One of three girls who I'd noticed seemed like friends raised her hand.

"Excellent, Scholar!" Mr. Grindle said, giving her a one-man round of applause.

"See?" Hogue whispered to me. "He really *doesn't* know anyone's name!"

The volunteer Scholar stood and—with a pretty good voice—began singing a song I'm pretty sure I'd never heard before.

> *If I ever had to choose*
> *The people of greatest worth*
> *No matter what I had to lose,*
> *I'd choose the Scholars of True North!*

The rest of the Scholars and Mr. Grindle joined in for the chorus.

> *Everybody clap your hands today!*
> *Sing it loud enough they hear you far away!*
> *Give us all your hoots, give us all your hollers!*

Nothing beats the spirit of
True North Scholars!

It went on for three more verses.

Naturally, as Rising Scholars, it was our job to collect everyone's sandwich wrappers and take them to the dump. Then it was back to work.

The trips from the stacks to the scanners, and from the scanners to the dump, and from the dump to the freight elevator, all blurred together. The older Scholar told me we would work until three o'clock. But that wasn't much help, because with no phone or watch, I couldn't tell what time it was. The room had no clocks.

After about two more hours—maybe three, who knows?— Karla and I found ourselves at the bins at the same time.

"Look at this," she whispered. She slid a document from the bottom of the stack she was about to dump: a birth certificate, dated forty-three years earlier. The baby's first name: LAWRENCE. His last name: EASTON.

"Whoa, cool," I said quietly. "I didn't know Mr. Easton was born here."

"Yep," she said. "And look at this."

She pointed to the line where the baby's middle name was typed in all caps:

BIRDWELL

CHAPTER
24

"**S**o what?" Jared said.

It was that afternoon and we were back on the bus, re-tracing our route from that morning. The sights of Leonard-ville passed by the bus window in reverse order, and with a thousand-percent brighter sunlight.

I liked it better at dawn.

Mr. Grindle sat two rows away, but the constant grind of the bus engine allowed us to talk in private.

Karla had snuck Mr. Easton's birth certificate out of the building under her blue shirt. She passed it to the others, who hadn't seen it yet, but Jared wasn't impressed.

"Don't you think it's weird?" I said.

"Maybe, but it doesn't mean anything," Jared said.

"He could be one of them!" Karla said. "The family who helped found the town."

"There aren't any of *them* left," Pratchett said. "That's the point of the whole Birdwell story. Abraham had no heirs, so he left his land to the city to make the park."

"Then why does he have that middle name?" Karla said.

"Who knows?" Jared said. "My middle name's Ford, but it doesn't mean I own a truck factory."

"Your middle name's Eugene," Hogue said.

"But it might as *well* be Ford!" Jared said. "You're proving my point for me."

"Well," Karla said, reaching under her shirt once more, "then why did his ancestors *also* have the middle name Birdwell?"

She passed two more documents across the aisle.

"What the heck, Karla?" I hissed. "How many of these did you steal?"

"We're throwing them away!" Karla said. "You can't *steal* trash!"

The more I got to know Karla Woo, the more I liked her.

Jared unfolded the papers. One of them was a birth certificate like Mr. Easton's, but older-looking. The other was a page torn from a book. They said that Mr. Easton's father's name was William Birdwell Easton, his paternal grandfather's name was Dwight Birdwell Easton, and his paternal great-grandfather's name was Morris Birdwell Easton.

"That's as far back as the records in the basement go," Karla said.

"Then I guess we'll never know," Jared said.

"What do you mean?" Karla said. "We can go ask him if he's a real Birdwell."

"Are you *insane*?" Jared said, a little too loud. "They're already using *us* to try to get him fired. If we want to help him, we should stay a hundred miles away."

Karla admitted she hadn't thought of that.

"If only there were some other way to find out," Pratchett said.

Jared said, "They should have a building where you can just go and find stuff out about the past."

"That would be awesome," Hogue said. "Like, anything you want to know, they would have books there to tell you."

"It should all be organized like the internet, so you can find the thing you're looking for," I said.

"Maybe have a helper there, too," Pratchett said. "Someone who knows the whole place inside out."

"That would be epic," Jared said.

"We should invent that when we're older," Hogue said.

"Totally," Pratchett said.

Just then, the bus bumped over a pothole in front of the Leonardville Public Library.

I looked at Jared. Jared looked at Pratchett. Pratchett looked at Hogue. Hogue looked at Karla.

"You guys are joking, right?" Karla said.

"Pshhhh, yeah," Hogue said. "Total joke."

We all nodded, but I don't think she believed us.

We arranged to go after school the next day. I told my parents I had to research a project on local history, which happened to be the truth.

"They don't have a library at True North?" my mom said. "Ooooh, how revolutionary."

Getting there took additional planning, since we weren't allowed to hang out together. If our parents dropped us all at the library, they'd spot each other. The only way was to ride our bikes to school so we could go to the library on our own afterward.

"You *want* to ride your bike at zero-dark-thirty?" my mom said. "Be my guest."

I don't think she completely trusted me, but her suspicion couldn't compete with her desire to stay in bed for another hour.

Remote Team the next day went mostly like the day before. The main difference was, when Beef Squad dropped our phones into the tub at six-forty-five, our fingers were bone-white from the chilly morning ride. It took an hour of hauling documents in the county building basement for the feeling in my hands to totally come back.

Lunch was ham sandwiches on the same white buns. A volunteer Scholar led us in another True North spirit song that had a different tune and different words but was somehow exactly the same. Then we rode back.

We didn't talk much, but then, we never do when we have a secret mission planned.

That's how far Beef Squad had fallen: our secret mission was a trip to the library with a girl who couldn't stand us.

"Great work today, Remote Team!" Mr. Grindle shouted from the front of the bus when we pulled into True North Academy for Excellence at three-thirty.

My legs, back, shoulders, and neck disagreed.

"I never thought I'd say this," Hogue said, standing at the bike racks and pushing his thumbs into his lower back, "but I miss LBJ."

"I thought my arms were going to fall off today," Jared said.

"Well, look on the bright side," Karla said. "Misty said we'll only be Rising Scholars for four or five months. Six, max."

"Wait," Jared said, snapping his helmet strap. "You're riding *that*?"

"What?" Karla said. "You mean my bike?"

"You call that a bike?" Jared said.

Karla sat on a purple BMX bike with white tires, a white seat, white pedals, white pads, shiny streamers coming out of the grips, and a racing placard on the bars. Instead of a racing number, it had shiny letters that spelled "Karla." The letters turned into rainbows when the light caught them.

"You call *that* a bike?" Karla said, nodding to Jared's used mountain bike. "Did you throw it off a building, or did it come pre-run-over?"

"This," Jared said, "is a chromoly-steel—"

But Karla was already rolling out into the street.

"You can tell me all about it," she said, "if you can catch me."

He never did.

Picture in your head the classic American library: brick steps leading up to a heavy wooden door, stone columns holding up a vaulted ceiling, and rows of bookshelves so deep they swallow the light.

Well, that's totally irrelevant, because the Leonardville Public Library is a double-wide trailer.

"It was supposed to be temporary," my dad explained once.

"And it still is," my mom said.

When we pushed through the door, Night Train was sitting at the library's computer, playing an online crossword game.

"Ancillary!" he shouted, typing in a flurry.

Night Train was no stranger to us. In this town, kids and homeless people end up in a lot of the same places. We'd see him in parks, in alleys, and under bridges. Nice guy.

"What's good, Train?" Jared said as he went inside.

"They chased me outta Birdwell again," Night Train said. "Got all manner a' people settin' up for the big shindig."

That's right—Pyrite Days was starting the following day. Between my early wake-ups and working in a basement, it had slipped my mind.

Hogue and Night Train traded their customary greeting:

two fist bumps followed by a thumb to the nose with wiggly fingers.

"Never change, Hogue," Night Train said.

"Never change, Night Train," Hogue answered.

"Well, it's good to see you—" Pratchett began saying, but Night Train threw up a hand. He'd gotten a new crossword clue.

"'A holla in La Scala,'" Night Train read aloud.

"Bravo," Karla said, following Pratchett into the library.

"Bravo back atcha!" Night Train said, typing the word.

Karla turned to the librarian, who sat behind a horseshoe-shaped desk reading *Anna Karenina.* She didn't look up until Karla spoke to her.

"Hi," Karla said. "We'd like to see the records from old Leonardville. The older, the better."

"Gilgamesh!" Night Train shouted behind us.

"I—I'm sorry," the librarian said. "You want to *see* something?" Her eyebrows bent down in confusion. She was younger than most of our teachers. Her hair was the color of the plums in the orchards by the river. She was dressed neatly but in a style I don't think Vice Principal Hopper would have allowed: jeans and a black T-shirt that said "I Became a Librarian for the Money—The Fame and Power Were Just Bonuses." A rectangular pin on her shirt gave her name as Joanne.

"Yeah," Karla said. "Old birth and death records, if you've got 'em."

"Is there a problem?" Pratchett said.

Her face softened into a disbelieving smile. "Problem? No—I'm thrilled! It's just been a while. Most kids come for the computer. Here, follow me."

The prefabricated floor shook beneath our feet as we all strode past the display of pyrite nuggets. The library did double duty as the local-history museum. Maybe that was why they'd splurged on a double-wide.

Joanne stopped at a large metal cabinet, which she unlocked with a key from her belt. Inside were about a hundred crusty-looking old books and maybe a dozen boxes.

"This is our earliest stuff," she said. "You gotta put these on to handle anything." She passed us a basket of cotton gloves.

"Cool! Like for old comic books," Hogue said.

"Yeah!" the librarian said. "Do you collect?"

"Yep," Hogue said. "But only the ones my dad buys."

"Aha," she said. "So *he* collects and you *steal* them."

"A hundred percent," Hogue said.

"Mississippi!" Night Train shouted.

Joanne pulled down a heavy volume and blew the dust off. "These are the only copies of these documents," she said. "The county is paying millions to some hotshot outfit to digitize their records and then ship the originals off to storage. They're going at a snail's pace. I don't know when they'll get around to this stuff."

We looked at one another. The hotshot outfit was *us*! But the only place we were shipping things was to the trash.

"Mulligatawny!" Night Train blurted out from behind us.

"What are you looking for particularly?" Joanne asked.

"Birth records from the 1850s," Karla said.

Joanne pulled down a different volume. She turned and laid it on a table. She opened the cover and began flipping through page after yellow page of names and dates inked in a stately cursive hand.

"These pages are mostly death records," she said, almost to herself, "'cause of the influenza outbreak of 1851."

"Hold on," Pratchett said. "Is that when all the Birdwells died?"

"Largemouth!" Night Train shouted.

"Well, not *all* of them," Joanne said. Then she stabbed a gloved finger onto one line. "Here—Augustus Birdwell. That was Abraham Birdwell's dad."

"Excuse me," Pratchett said, nudging her out of the way. He already had his phone in hand.

"What are you doing?" Joanne said.

"Digitizing your records," Pratchett said. He framed up the page in his screen and snapped a photo. Then he snapped one of the next page, then the next page, and the next. In less than ten minutes he had made a high-resolution copy of the whole book.

"Thank you," Pratchett said, closing the volume. "We're done here. Would you like a set of the files? I can send them on FaceGram."

"Um, I'm not on FaceGram," Joanne said.

"I don't blame you," Pratchett said. "It's a huge time-suck. InstaBook?"

"No," Joanne said.

"Right," Pratchett said. "'Cause of all the security breaches. Bok-Bok?"

"*Bok-Bok?*" the librarian repeated. "Can you just email it to me?"

"Dangit, I'm not on that one," Pratchett said. "My mom is, though. I'll send the files to her Bok-Bok and she can email them from there."

"Dogleg!" Night Train shouted.

"Can you keep it down, Night Train?" Joanne said. "This is a library, after all."

"Is it?" Night Train said. "Looks like a trailer to me. Should see the library in Vienna. Makes this place look like an outhouse."

"I'm sure it does," she said, shaking her head.

We were walking toward the door when Hogue said, "Hey, I have a donation. It's for the pyrite collection." He held out the gold-colored lump of metal he'd retrieved from the drill in the park.

"Cool!" Joanne said, weighing the heft of it in her hand. "I'll leave it with a note for Sally."

"Who's Sally?" Hogue said.

"The curator of the exhibits," Joanne said. "She handles all the donations."

"Where is she now?" Hogue said.

"Not here," Joanne said. "But I'm sure she'll be thrilled."

"What if she's not?" Hogue said.

"Sorry?" Joanne said.

"What if she's not thrilled?" Hogue said. "What if we catch her on a bad day, or what if she's so in love with the pyrite that's already here that she doesn't want to ruin it by adding a new piece of pyrite? A million things could happen. Then I just gave my pyrite away for nothing."

The librarian nodded politely in the way I've seen countless grown-ups nod when talking to Hogue.

Our friend went on: "What, exactly, would you say in this so-called note to Sally?"

"Uhhhhh," Joanne said. "You know, just, 'Here's some pyrite a local boy found.'"

"That's it?" Hogue said. "Don't you think you can do better than that?"

"Would you like to write the note?" Joanne said, reaching to her desk for a pad. "I'm sure Sally would love to hear directly from you."

"Me?" Hogue said. "What would *I* say? I don't know this woman. I've never met Sally in my life!"

Just when I was sure the librarian was starting to question her choice of career, Night Train stepped in.

"I'll take your pyrite, little man," he said.

"Thank you," Hogue said, taking the rock out of Joanne's hand and passing it to our homeless friend.

"No, thank *you,*" Night Train said, inspecting the gift under a reading lamp.

"See?" Hogue said to the librarian. "*That's* the polite way to accept a gift."

"Nah, I can't take it," Night Train said, offering it back to Hogue.

"Don't tell me," Hogue said. "You need Sally's permission, too?"

"Nah," Night Train said. "It just wouldn't be right."

"It's right if I'm *giving* it to you," Hogue said. "Please, Night Train, take my pyrite."

"That's the thing, son," Night Train said. "I can't take it 'cause it ain't pyrite."

We all leaned forward to get a better look at the yellow nugget in Hogue's hand.

"This right here?" Night Train said. "Pure gold."

"Well, in that case," Hogue said, "I insist you take it."

CHAPTER
25

"**E**ight ounces of gold! That's like ten thousand dollars!" Mad Jared said. "You could have been rich!"

We were outside the library minutes later. We had already said goodbye to Night Train, who headed up the Esplanade toward the bank.

(Joanne, the librarian who had just turned down a solid-gold nugget, followed us onto the sidewalk, watched Night Train walk away, then went back inside without saying a word. I wonder how often she still thinks about it.)

"What do I want with ten thousand dollars?" Hogue said. "I can't even buy video games until my parents unground me."

"Give it to me!" Mad Jared said. "Ten grand could have made us *professionals*! We could have bought the radios the Navy SEALs use! Or minibikes for everyone! Or third-gen night vision! Or—"

He was too frustrated to finish the thought. He just looked up at the sky, as if watching a flock of third-generation night-vision goggles fly away toward the horizon.

"Night Train needs the money more than you guys do," Karla said.

"That's a good point, I guess," I said. Until then I'd been on Mad Jared's side.

"What does Night Train need Navy SEAL radios for?" Mad Jared said.

"He needs a *house*," Karla shot back.

"*Ghaaaaaa!*" Mad Jared said, grabbing his head.

"Guys, that gold nugget's already helped us plenty," Pratchett said.

"How?" Hogue said.

"Yeah, how?" I said.

"This I'd like to hear," Mad Jared said.

Pratchett looked at us for a few seconds.

"I don't know," he said.

It was the first time I'd ever heard Pratchett say those three words in that particular order.

"I just know it helped us somehow," he said. "I'll have to think it through some more."

"Awesome!" Mad Jared said. "That's what I'll tell them over at Cobra Advanced Optics when they ask how I'm paying for four night-vision headsets. 'Don't worry, Neil. My friend Pratchett says we're all good; he just needs to think about it some more.'"

Karla asked the question we were all thinking.

"Are you really on first-name basis with a military contractor?"

"I can't help it if I'm *friendly*!" Mad Jared said.

We split up for the ride home, just in case someone's parents happened to drive by. When I turned onto Marlow Street, I rode right past my house. I kept on riding to the park.

True to Night Train's word, Birdwell Park was buzzing. Workers were erecting the stage and video screen at the eastern edge of the field. Another crew was using a forklift to unload portable toilets next to the restroom. Dozens of vendors were setting up tents and tables on what would be the midway. In addition, the Placid Meadow drilling crew was there again. This time they had set up on the opposite corner, not far from the twenty-point sprinkler in Stupidball. The drill bit made a grinding roar, like a blender full of rocks.

With all that going on, the last thing I noticed was the new billboard welcoming park visitors from the little parking lot. It read:

• PARK RENOVATION COMING •

New Playground! Improved Tennis Courts! Competition Basketball Court!

A Generous Gift from Your Friends at

PLACID MEADOW CONSTRUCTION CO.

"God, I love this town," said a voice behind me.

I turned around. Officer Jim leaned against the passenger-side door of his cruiser and smiled. The drill noise had covered the sound of his engine as he approached. It occurred to me that he must have known it would.

I nodded.

"How you liking the new joint?" he said, stepping forward to stand beside me. "I hear great things about what Paula and Greg are doing over there."

Paula and Greg were Head Smith and Mr. Grindle. I had picked up that much in our first days.

"It's good," I said. "We're on Remote Team. Just Rising Scholars for now, but in five or six months we'll probably be High Achievers. Maybe even Ring of Excellence Honorees."

Officer Jim nodded.

"You probably think I don't notice that tone you're using," he said. "Repeating Paula and Greg's words like I can't hear the sarcasm? Most grown-ups probably can't. I bet that gives you a real good feeling. Kinda like you can see us, but we can't see you."

I swallowed hard.

"I want you to think real good about your attitude," he said. "True North is your last shot, son. You get the boot there, I don't know what happens to Nick Rhodes and the Beef Squad. And poor Karla Woo—" He whistled like a boiling kettle. "Worst mistake of her life, falling in with you guys. Spare a thought for her, eh?"

He took another look out over the park.

"Yep, it's all gonna work out fine if you just let it be," he said. He nodded once—like punctuation—then walked around to the driver's side of the cruiser.

"Oh, I almost forgot," he said. "About an hour ago, the school board fired Lawrence Easton. You and your friends' interviews were key to their decision, so please pass along my gratitude."

He put his hands together and bowed in thanks, then got into the cruiser and drove away.

I took out my phone and texted Beef Squad. The message was just one word:

ANTIDISESTABLISHMENTARIANISM

No replies came. None were expected.

Just over six hours later, at ten minutes to midnight, I slid my window open and listened to the tree frogs' serenade. I took some comfort in knowing that they would be singing again the following night.

But would I be here to listen to them?

I climbed out my window and down my no-longer-secret ladder in the ivy. I rode my bike to the Esplanade Bridge and took the twelve steps down onto the pebble beach. This was the place where Beef Squad promised to meet, no questions asked, if anyone raised the alarm. In the moonlight I counted three silhouettes.

They had come.

"Did you hear about Easton?" Pratchett said.

"Yeah, but that's just part of it," I said. "I figured it all out."

"What?" Hogue said.

"The nugget," I said. "Pratchett was right. It's already given us everything we need to help Mr. Easton."

"For ten grand?" Jared said. "I hope so."

"Paul Dekker says he's going to renovate Birdwell Park, but he's not," I said. "He's going to *mine* it. Strip out the gold—millions of dollars' worth, probably—right under the city's nose. Then he'll jet off to the Maldives, where he just bought a house."

"That's where Scott's gecko came from," Hogue said, recalling the confrontation in the park two weeks ago.

It felt like two years ago.

"Criminals can't be extradited from the Maldives," Pratchett said. "He could live the rest of his life there as a millionaire."

"Wait," Hogue said. "How does he know there's gold in the park? I didn't tell anyone where I found the nugget."

"He's been drilling holes in the place for the last month," I said. "That can't be the only nugget they found."

"Did they just get lucky?" Jared said.

"They've known the gold was there for two years," I said.

"How do you figure—" Jared started.

"The expressway," Pratchett said, interrupting. "Placid Meadow dug the cut. Of course!"

I nodded, but I didn't know if anyone could see it in the dark.

"Those weasels!" Jared said. "How did they keep that a secret for two whole years?"

"Probably by promising their crew a portion of whatever they find," I said.

"Just like Eustace Leonard," Pratchett said.

"Gold does crazy things to people," I said. "If it didn't, this town wouldn't even exist."

"Okay," Hogue said. "How does Mr. Easton fit into all this?"

"It's still just a hunch," I said. "But we've got the whole night to prove it."

"Then let's prove it," Hogue said.

"I'm in," Pratchett said.

"Hold on," Jared said. "Are we going to get arrested again?"

"You better hope not," I said. "Because we're going to your house."

CHAPTER
26

It was the biggest Pyrite Days ever.

Just past eleven in the morning, Birdwell Park was a sea of ball caps with some trees and a concert stage rising in their midst. My parents and I watched a truck inch through the crowd with six additional Porta-Potties.

"There were guys just peeing onto the expressway," a man next to us said. "It was like San Francisco!"

"Really?" my mom said. "When's the last time you were in San Francisco?"

The guy didn't answer.

"That's what I thought," she said.

That morning, for the first time in my life, I had skipped the Pyrite Days parade. We'd been up all night in Jared's dad's office, so sleeping in was a no-brainer. The funny thing was, I didn't care that I'd missed it. I wondered if I would ever get up early for it again.

"I'm going to go buy something," I said to my parents.

"Don't spend your money all in one place," my dad said.

"Why not?" I said.

My dad didn't answer.

"That's what I thought," I said, grinning.

Dad smiled back at me.

"Meet us for lunch at noon," he said.

"Oh, you'll see me then," I said.

As I pressed through the people, I detected a charge in the air—an electric feeling of possibility. Or maybe my head was just frazzled from lack of sleep. The five of us had worked until five a.m. Mr. Tamblyn's engineering workspace was in their garage, so Jared's family didn't have to listen to our slap-happy arguments through the night.

After climbing back through my window, I'd been so excited that it took me an hour to fall asleep.

As far as Beef Squad missions go, this was a piece of cake. I was actually surprised we hadn't thought of something like it sooner. The stakes, however, were exponentially higher than ever before. That's why Pratchett took the precaution of texting us the timetable.

"Dekker plans to make millions off that park," Pratchett said. "All those people celebrating there will make him nervous. His guys will be on the lookout for anything strange, weird, or disturbing."

"Like us!" Hogue said.

Since everyone in town was suspicious of us, we'd have to pull it all off together but separately. We would enter the park at different times and from different directions.

My main worry was that Jared would oversleep, since no one would be going by to roust him from bed.

The jumbotron over the stage showed the band. They wore the formal concert apparel of Leonardville grown-ups: T-shirts, baggy shorts, and hiking sandals. The electric guitarist was a clean-shaven guy who never once opened his eyes. He was at least five minutes into a solo and looked to be just warming up.

I walked onto the crowded midway. Booths lined the walkway to my left and right. Some offered games like ring-toss and bobbing for apples. Others sold crafts and food. The grilled corn looked delicious, but the smoke from the coals stung my eyes.

"Face painting!" a man shouted from a booth up ahead. "Getcha pretty face painted here!"

I turned into his booth. The man looked me over.

"You want your face painted?" he asked, sounding skeptical. I didn't know his name, but I knew he ran the youth drama company, Beehive Theatre. Hogue had done some shows with Beehive when he was younger, and we'd all gone to watch. In one play, this man had played Sasquatch, but he'd played him with an English accent, which was super funny.

"Yes, please," I said.

"Lots of older kids coming by today," he said, taking my money. "Must be a meme or something. Is it a meme?"

"Yeah, no," I said. "I don't know. Maybe?"

"I think that's every answer," the man said. "Olivia's got you right here."

He pointed to an open chair by a high school–aged girl. It was one of four chairs around a big table of makeup and face paint.

Olivia didn't seem surprised to see me at all.

"Let me guess," she said when I sat down. "A Protector from *Dynamus*?"

I smiled. "Level 129 Scout, please."

Ten minutes later she still wasn't done.

"How's it coming, Olivia?" the man said. "We got customers."

"Almost," Olivia said, penciling in the lines around my mouth.

"Do you play?" I asked.

"Don't move," she said. "Level 67 Trailblazer. I've been stuck on Moons of Thor since Christmas."

I nodded.

"Don't move," she said. "The Meat Wizard is bumming me out. He's got to be the worst boss in the game." She put the pencil down. "You are done, Protector."

She handed me a mirror.

It was amazing. My entire face, from my chin to my hairline and across both ears, was painted in different shades of red. Black pencil lines demarcated the armor plates. She'd even drawn little hinge pins for my jaw. I *was* a Protector.

"Okay, musical chairs time," the man said, guiding a five-year-old girl toward us.

I stood up and turned to Olivia. "There's a door on the wrecked shuttle that says 'Push.'"

"Yeah," she said. "It's locked. *And* grenade-proof. Believe me, I tried it."

I nodded. "Next time, try *pulling.*"

She closed her eyes for a moment and smiled like a statue of a Buddha, a vision of pure serenity. Then she spoke.

"I hate that freakin' game with every freakin' fiber of my being."

We've all been there. I waved goodbye to Olivia and turned back onto the midway. Our plan was to wear clothes we didn't normally wear. I had on an old Giants World Series T-shirt that I usually slept in. On my way to the bandstand I passed the skaters coming the other way. I made eye contact with Jesse Concepción, but he looked right past me.

The face paint worked.

Good thing, too, because the next person I recognized was Officer Jim. He led two other cops down the midway directly toward me. He smiled broadly to the townspeople on his left and right as he passed them.

I'd used to think he smiled like a golden retriever. Now I knew he smiled like a crocodile.

As Officer Jim got closer, he looked straight at me. My brain told me that if Jesse didn't recognize me, then Officer Jim wouldn't either. But my nerves couldn't take it. I turned away and found myself faced with a rack of sock puppets. I grabbed the nearest one—a frog with a big red mouth.

"I know who you are," a woman said.

It was the puppet maker, watching me from her lawn chair.

"It's so obvious, you can't hide it!" she said.

She wore a blue windbreaker and sandals. Her feet were so dirty it was hard to see where they stopped and the real dirt started.

I'd never seen her before in my life. How did she recognize me?

The cops were just a few steps away.

"You are *obviously* . . . a boy who loves puppets!" she said, smiling big.

Her teeth looked like an ice-cube tray with half the cubes taken.

Officer Jim and the two other cops passed by, continuing their slow patrol down the midway. I returned the puppet to the rack and hurried in the opposite direction.

"But that frog needs a friend!" the puppet lady shouted after me.

"Sorry, frog!" I called over my shoulder.

Onstage, the guitarist was maybe almost done with his solo but also maybe not even halfway done. The screen over the stage showed a close-up of his face. He cringed with each note, twisting his head back and forth. If I didn't know better, I would have guessed he was sticking his hand into a clogged toilet.

According to the graphic on the kick drum, this band was called the Cantaloupe Locomotive. Their music wasn't much better than their name, but it was good enough to get fifteen or twenty people dancing in front of the stage, raising a haze of dust that gave a sepia color to the whole scene.

Just like a photo from the Gold Rush, I thought.

I turned behind me to the sound table, which was manned by a guy with no hair on his head but a full-on jungle all over his face. It was one of those beards that went up almost to his lower eyelids, like some gland in his body was pumping out too much of something.

"How much longer for these guys?" I yelled, casually laying my left hand on his table.

He shrugged like it was a stupid question. "It's rock 'n' roll," he shouted.

"How can you tell?" I shouted back. He gave me a dirty look, which made it easy to push the dongle into a port on the side of his mixing board without him noticing.

"It'll be over when it's over," he said.

I nodded and turned back around. After a few more minutes of guitar solo, I noticed a boy on the far side of the dancers with his face painted like a Level-131 Scout.

I gave Hogue a nod. He nodded back.

Our plan put an awful lot of trust in Beehive Theatre's face-painting booth.

There was still no sign of Jared, though. And he had the most important job of all.

I checked my watch. The band was supposed to have been done playing ten minutes ago. Jared was late, but this solo had taken on a life of its own. Now the guy had the guitar behind his back, and he was playing scales and jiggling his face so his cheeks shook like jelly.

I looked over at Hogue. He shrugged.

Just then, a screech of microphone feedback rang out from the speakers.

"Check, check, check," came a voice. No one onstage was speaking. Someone had turned on another microphone.

Mayor Karl stepped from behind the backdrop.

According to my dad, Mayor Karl wasn't really that powerful. "Figurehead" was the word he used. Mayor Karl did not inspire confidence. He wore his straw-colored hair parted down the middle, like there was a zipper on his head someone had accidentally left open. Even though he was mayor, he wore shorts and sandals, just like the Cantaloupe Locomotive.

As he walked out to the front of the stage, the band showed no sign of stopping. Not even with the mayor of the city interrupting them on his own microphone.

"Okay, how about that?" Mayor Karl said to the crowd, awkwardly clapping for the musicians so that his mic went *pop-pop-pop-pop-pop-pop*. Another cycle of feedback rang out over the park.

People covered their ears.

The guitarist kicked it into an even higher gear. He had the guitar running between his legs. He played the fingerboard on the front side and picked the strings back behind his thigh. It was kind of amazing.

I was starting to like the Cantaloupe Locomotive.

Mayor Karl regrouped and tried again.

"Let's hear it for Leonardville's own Honeydew Freight Train!" he said.

"Wrong!" a woman in front of me shouted.

"Oh, gosh," Mayor Karl said. "They told me it was something like that."

"Let 'em play!" came a deep voice from the back.

"Yeah!" shouted a woman over on Hogue's side of the dance pit. "We're rockin' here!"

"I get that," Mayor Karl said. "And believe me, no one loves rockin' more than this guy, hey-hey?"

"So SHUT UP!" a man in the middle of the dance pit bellowed.

Was this scene about to get ugly? All because the guitarist for the Cantaloupe Locomotive wanted to take an epic twenty-five-minute guitar solo?

Thankfully, no. Because right then, the drummer hit a loud beat on his snare. That was the cue. They played one towering chord, over which the guitarist continued noodling. Then another, then another. They were building up to something big.

"Oh, my!" Mayor Karl said.

A quick drumroll sent the Cantaloupe Locomotive to their last chord, which was short and punchy, like a gunshot.

The song was finally over. The dancers cheered as the band walked off the stage.

The Pyrite Days program was moving on.

Where was Jared? My worst fear was coming true—he had overslept.

"As I'm sure you've heard," Mayor Karl said, "Birdwell Park, here, is about to get a major face-lift. A total renovation. It's thanks to the generosity of one man. A pillar of our city and an example for us all. Please join me in welcoming to the stage Mr. Paul Dekker!"

He did the *pop-pop-pop-pop-pop-pop* thing again, which triggered another round of feedback.

People covered their ears.

As I watched Mr. Dekker step up to the front of the stage, I was brainstorming backup plans. The Almond Festival was in October. Maybe we could postpone the mission till then. I was thinking so hard I almost didn't notice the Level 143 Heavy walk behind the stage.

Jared had made it after all.

It turns out he *did* sleep in, but he woke up just in time.

When it was all over, the rest of us had to admit his timing was perfect.

CHAPTER

27

Mr. Dekker wore khaki pants and a good white shirt. Looking more mayoral than the real mayor, he plucked a microphone from its stand.

"You people know me. I was born and raised here in Leonardville. I'm proud to be raising my own son here. I'm happy to see that it's turning him into a fine young man. A *fine* young man."

An obnoxiously loud cough was audible from behind the stage as Jared made his objection known.

"People come up to me and say, 'Paul, what are you, crazy? Everything you do makes money. You're gonna spend all this dough on a *gift*? You're gonna do all this work for free? Hire all these tradesmen? Buy all this lumber? For nothing?' I say to them, 'No, my friend, not for nothing—'"

Suddenly his mic cut out as hundreds of watts of white noise crashed through the speakers. The fuzz only lasted for a split second, because the video screen blinked to life with something that looked and sounded exactly like a historical documentary film. Images of old Leonardville faded in and out. A soft banjo tune played while Hogue's voice boomed out across the park.

"Everyone knows the story of Birdwell Park. Abraham Birdwell donated his land to the city because he had no heir to pass it on to. But what if—"

Here he stopped for a loud record scratch.

"—that wasn't true, and there *is* an heir?"

Jared must have really jacked up the volume, because Hogue's narration thundered like the voice of Zeus. Suddenly people were crowding in from the booths and the picnic area to see what was going on. I noticed our parents among them, stepping closer from the refreshment truck.

Onstage, Mr. Dekker was shouting over the crowd to the man at the sound table.

"Cut it off!" he said.

"I'm not playing it!" the bearded man said, raising his palms upward.

I almost felt bad for the tech guy. Minutes earlier, backstage, Jared had unplugged the input cable and replaced it with one that ran to his phone. The dongle I had slyly plugged into the public address system made a wireless connection to the phone, so none of the sound man's channels were working. We had hijacked the entire system with one phone and a few pieces of cast-off junk from Jared's dad's desk drawer.

The narration began again as the image changed. It was close-up shots of birth records Pratchett had photographed in the library.

"Ladies and gentlemen," Hogue's recorded voice said through the speakers, "there *are* heirs to the Birdwell name. They start with the child of Abraham's brother, Conrad, who was born out of wedlock."

A gasp went up from the crowd. I like to think it was because they were shocked by the news and not because they were uptight about that kind of thing.

"The records in the Leonardville Public Library prove that the name lives on to this day. Dwight Birdwell Easton was the father of William Birdwell Easton. And *he* was father of Lawrence Birdwell Easton."

The birth certificates dissolved into a smiling portrait from the LBJ yearbook.

"Isn't that the teacher they just fired?" a guy in a beer T-shirt shouted.

"What?" a young woman yelled. "I *love* Mr. Easton!"

"Totally!" came a man's voice from the back. "He's the best teacher in that school!"

Hogue's recorded voice went on. "Upon seeing such a loaded history, you won't be surprised to learn that the stated reason for Mr. Easton's firing was total and complete—"

People gasped louder when they heard the word Hogue said. I'm not proud of it, but in our defense, we'd written the script at three a.m. Maybe our judgment was failing.

But it worked.

Mr. Dekker leapt off the stage, batting his beloved towns-people aside as he sprinted for the sound table. He ran right past me, grabbed the sound board's power cable, and ripped it out of the nearby generator. That would have killed the public address system dead, ending our mission, except that about a half hour earlier, Pratchett—painted to look like a Level-174 Demolisher—had plugged a different extension cord into the other side of the PA. That cord ran to a generator sitting on the back of a taco truck whose owners had no idea they were sending power to the stage.

"What's going on?" Mr. Dekker demanded of the sound man.

"I don't know, but you're blocking my view," the sound man said. "Are you watching this? It's *crazy.*"

"No, no, no, no, no!" Mr. Dekker said, sprinting back toward the stage.

"But here's the coolest part," Hogue's voice said. "The reason they had to get Mr. Easton out of town, and the reason Mr. Dekker is suddenly *sooooo* worked up to do a big construction job for free—"

This was it: the big revelation. The discovery that tied it all together. It was going to solve all our problems and maybe even reverse our town's bad fortune.

That was when the screen went dark and the speakers fell silent.

Standing below the screen, Officer Jim was removing his finger from the one control we had no way to hijack: the panel's on-off button. In his other hand, Officer Jim clamped

Jared's upper arm. Even through his face paint I could see how heartbroken Jared looked.

"Hey, we were watching that," the man in the beer T-shirt yelled.

"*That,*" Officer Jim said, in an easygoing tone, "was a crime committed against this town."

"We want to see what it says!" a woman shouted.

"It's just more slander, more made-up hoo-ha," Officer Jim said. He looked right at me. "Will you guys please grab me *that* one?"

Suddenly I was seized from behind by a policeman I didn't know was there.

"Aaaaaaaaaaand *that* one," Officer Jim said, pointing at Hogue. Another officer took him by the arm. They marched us up through the crowd.

I couldn't believe how close we had come. I couldn't believe how much trouble we were in. I couldn't believe how bad all those dancers *stank.* Oh, my god, they smelled bad.

We stepped onto the stage. From up there I could see all our parents. The color had drained from their faces. My dad dropped his forehead onto his hand.

"There's a fourth out there somewhere," Officer Jim said. "Look for another boy with robot makeup."

The two cops fanned out into the crowd to search for Pratchett.

We were onstage with Officer Jim, Mr. Dekker, and Mayor Karl. The mayor had kept silent so far, but he spoke up now.

"What's going on here, Paul?" he said to Mr. Dekker.

"We've caught some conspirators," Officer Jim said, as if the question had been directed at him. "It'll just be a moment till we find the last one."

"No, I mean, what was *that*?" he said, pointing to the video screen. "Did you know Larry Easton was a Birdwell?"

"Just play the movie!" a woman yelled from over near my mother.

No, wait—that *was* my mother.

Others joined her.

Officer Jim let go of Jared's arm and stepped forward.

"Folks! Folks!" he said. "This is all nothing but a big prank pulled by these kids."

"Oh, baloney!" Hogue's dad shouted. "Play the video!"

"Play it now!" Pratchett's mom yelled.

Someone struck up a chant, and the sea of townspeople quickly joined in.

"Play *it*! Play *it*! Play *it*!" they shouted.

Even Mayor Karl was chanting.

Officer Jim raised his eyes to the back of the crowd. "Aha! Excellent work, men!" he said.

The two other cops hustled up, each holding one arm of a Level-174 Demolisher: Pratchett. They'd gotten all of us. Pratchett was so crestfallen he looked twenty pounds lighter.

"The show is over," Officer Jim said. "Please disperse at once. This concludes Pyrite Days festivities for the current year. Anyone remaining on city property five minutes from now will be prosecuted to the fullest extent of the law."

"Oh, get a life," Pratchett's mom called out. Officer Jim ignored that.

The cops lifted Pratchett onto the stage surprisingly easily. That was when I noticed it wasn't Pratchett at all.

"Hey," Karla said, smiling through her *Dynamus* makeup.

Officer Jim was too busy trying to shoo people out of the park to notice that the boy his men had apprehended was actually a girl.

"What are you doing here?" Jared asked.

"When I heard the news about Easton getting fired, I was expecting a million texts from you guys," she said. "When I didn't get any, I got curious."

"So you hacked our phones," I said.

Karla shrugged.

"Did you really think I was going to miss my first real Beef Squad mission?"

"It was a good one," Hogue said. "Not quite good enough, but that's never stopped us."

"Nope," Karla said.

"Hold on," Jared said, fixing Karla with a look I could see through the paint. "You spied on *our* private communication, stole *our* plans, and showed up uninvited on *our* mission?"

Karla cocked her head defiantly.

"That," Jared said, "is the most Beef Squad thing I've ever heard. Welcome to the team."

He extended a fist.

"Thanks," Karla said, bumping it.

The crowd had resumed their chant.

"Play *it*! Play *it*! Play *it*!" they yelled, shaking their fists in unison.

Officer Jim was unmoved. He turned to the two other officers. "These boys are all repeat offenders," he said. "Take them straight to juvenile hall."

His eyes locked onto Karla. His mouth dropped open as he realized he'd been duped.

"Hey!" he said. "Where's the other boy?"

He grabbed Karla by her shoulders and bellowed in her face.

"Where! Is! He!"

The answer to that question has since grown into a legend. You'll hear people say Pratchett was way out past the picnic tables. Or even farther, in the parking lot. I even heard once that he was across the street, which I'm sure is not true.

What is true is that Pratchett was pretty dang far away when he threw the now-famous ear of roast corn.

Up onstage I recognized it at once: a tiny spindle-shaped projectile rising from back in the sycamores, tumbling end over end as it soared over the upraised fists of our neighbors.

I thought, *Huh, an ear of roast corn.*

I was as surprised as anyone when it covered the distance in less than a second. If Pratchett had been throwing it to me, I wouldn't have gotten my hands up in time to catch it.

But he wasn't.

He was aiming for the video screen. Specifically, the corner of the video screen that housed the on-off button.

And because, as you might recall, our friend Pratchett's left arm is a Gettysburg cannon, he did not miss.

What followed, in instant succession, were the *thwonk!* of the buttery corn hitting the panel and Hogue's supernaturally loud voice once again addressing the park full of townspeople.

"Leonardville is famous for our pyrite, so this will come as quite a surprise," he said.

Officer Jim went berserk. He pounded the video panel with his flashlight, but Pratchett's corncob fastball must have broken it in the "on" position.

"Please get ahold of yourself, Officer Leonard," the mayor said.

My friends and I traded astonished looks. Officer *Leonard*? As in, *that* Leonard? It was the first time we'd ever heard Officer Jim's last name. But our moment of discovery didn't last long.

"The ground under your feet?" the Hogue voice said as the video cut to an aerial image of Birdwell Park. "It's absolutely packed with real, genuine, twenty-four-karat gold!"

"Noooooooo!" Officer Jim bellowed. He spun around to face the town that bore his name. "The gold is mine! This whole park is mine! That judge never should have let them keep it! We won it fair and square!"

It was hard not to laugh, so we did.

"Hey, I'm getting some negative vibes, here," Hogue said to Officer Jim Leonard. "Remember, winners never whine—"

All five of us joined in for the punch line: *"And whiners never win!"*

Officer Jim snapped his head our way.

"You kids are monsters!" he hissed. *"Monsters!"*

"I guess you should have thought of that before you messed with Beef Squad," Jared said.

The video was wrapping up.

"That's the end, and the truth," Hogue's voice said. "Happy Pyrite Days, everyone, and thanks for listening!"

The screen went black. For a few seconds, all was quiet.

A woman way in back shouted, "Did he say gold?"

"There's gold in the park?" a man closer to us said.

"There's gold in the park!" someone yelled over by the booths.

Mr. Easton once showed us a movie about how nuclear chain reactions work. That's what the crowd of people in the park were like that day. Cries of "Gold!" rose all over the ten acres of Abraham Birdwell's former farm.

Then the man in the beer T-shirt fell to his hands and knees and clawed at the grass. People around him did the same.

"Please, folks!" Mayor Karl shouted. "Please! Aw, come on, guys!"

It was no use.

The grown-ups of Leonardville commenced tearing their park to shreds. Clumps of dirt and grass flew through the air like popcorn kernels exploding. I tried to find our parents in the scrum, but they were lost out there among the others, down on their knees, scraping through the earth with their fingernails.

Suddenly a man in a purple Sacramento Kings cap stood up, holding his hand high. "I got a nugget!" he shouted. "It's gold, baby! Gold, baby!"

That was the extent of his celebration, because fifty of his neighbors tackled him in a furious effort to relieve him of his gold baby.

"People!" Mayor Karl said, almost to himself. "Citizens!"

In the end, a fire truck rolled onto the upturned soil and sprayed the crowd down with a water cannon. The high-pressure shower finally snapped everyone out of their gold fever. They fled the park like stray dogs, some reaching down to grab a final clod of earth to take home.

We stood onstage with the mayor, watching it all.

The aftermath looked like a war zone: not a blade of grass in sight. The swing set lay on its side, as if it had been bombed by drones.

Mr. Dekker was nowhere to be seen. Officer Jim had likewise slipped away. Pratchett, coming from wherever he had been, stepped onto the stage without a word.

Hogue said, "I guess we should have kept our mouths shut about the gold."

"Who knew grown-ups could be such greedy ding-dongs?" Pratchett said.

"Oh, I could've told you that," Mayor Karl said.

"Well, look on the bright side," Jared said. "No more park?"

The four of us smiled, then said in unison: "No more Swimming Pool Contract!"

"What's a swimming-pool contract?" Karla asked.

"Yeah, what's a swimming-pool contract?" Mayor Karl asked.

CHAPTER
28

The water was freezing, but none of us cared. We were just happy to be at the first pool party of the season.

It was the day after the Big Dig, as the destruction of the park became known. Jared's parents' invitation was last-minute, so I was happy to see Karla, her parents, and her little sister come through the back gate. Mrs. Woo was even carrying a casserole dish.

For a beginner, Karla was surprisingly good at Death Squid Versus Machine-Gun Shark.

I took the pool party to be a kind of apology from our parents. They were sorry for not putting up a bigger fight against Officer Jim, who everyone now understood was just as corrupt as his great-great-great-grandfather Eustace Leonard. (It had taken Pratchett all of ten minutes with his photo records to confirm their relationship.) They were probably also ashamed of having acted like crazed greedheads and torn up the park with everyone else.

The barbecued chicken and cupcakes for dessert were meant to brush all that under the rug. Of course it worked. Once again, we forgave our parents for being less-than-perfect human beings. (All of us except Hogue, who said, "I play my cards right, I'll get a VR system out of this whole thing.")

We were making so much noise I'm surprised anyone heard the doorbell. But when Jared's dad led the new guest into the backyard, we all went quiet in a hurry.

He was a tall man with dark hair, and he was definitely not dressed for a pool party.

"Kids," Mr. Tamblyn said. "This is Detective Ramirez from the Leonardville PD. He'd like to talk."

"Sorry, hello!" my mom said, rising from her seat at the patio table. "Shouldn't they have lawyers present?"

"That's up to you, ma'am," Detective Ramirez said. "I can assure you these kids are not the target of my investigation."

The five of us, wrapped in colorful towels, sat around the table with the detective while our parents loomed over our shoulders.

Detective Ramirez told us that Officer Jim had been placed on leave while they investigated him. The police higher-ups felt that a cop who did something illegal was the worst kind of crook.

"You were right," he said. "He and Paul Dekker secretly

planned to mine gold from the park under the guise of a renovation project," he said.

"Shyeah," Jared said, with an edge in his voice. "That's what we *told* you!"

"He just *said* we were right!" I said.

Jared raised his hands in a sign of surrender.

"Well," Detective Ramirez said. "A lot of paperwork got signed that made no mention of gold mining, so that's fraud, which is a crime. There's also conspiracy."

"Hey!" Hogue said. "That's what Officer Jim said *we* did!"

"That's actually why I'm here," Detective Ramirez said. "There was a wild card Officer Jim and Paul Dekker were clearly worried about."

"Mr. Easton," Pratchett said.

The detective nodded.

"Officer Jim used you kids to get Mr. Easton fired so he would leave town. That way he'd be less likely to make a claim on the land as a Birdwell heir. Specifically, he and Mr. Dekker were waiting for you to enter Butte Nuggets Hall," he said.

"Hold on," my mom said. "How did they know the boys would be there that night?"

"They had the aid of a juvenile who delivered a message to your son," he said. "A message whose sole purpose was to get them all there under false pretenses."

"So in official police terms, we were set up?" I said, looking pointedly at my mom.

"You could say that," the detective said.

Mom rolled her eyes but then smiled at me. That's about as close as she's ever come to admitting she was wrong.

"Right now our priority is to nail down this case," Detective Ramirez said. "So in exchange for your cooperation, we will recommend that the DA not bring charges against you."

"Let's see if I have this straight," Hogue said. "You let us go scot-free, and we get to help you put Officer Jim in jail?"

"Pretty much," Detective Ramirez said.

Seeing all our smiles, he couldn't help breaking into one himself.

"Mom? Dad?" Jared said. "Get this man a cupcake."

The robot arm moved gracefully to the table, picked up the soup can, and pressed it into the electric can opener.

Then terrible things happened.

The angle was wrong, so the can spilled as the blade cut through. Gray broth covered the circuits, which shorted out the servos and caused the robot arm to press even harder. Sparks flew, and a grinding noise filled the gym as smoke rose from the arm's claw.

When the can finally fell from the arm's grip, a hundred parents watching from the bleachers let out a collective *"Awwwwww."*

The can rattled on the floor, dead. A chicken-noodle puddle spread out on the hardwood.

One of the judges rang the bell that signaled failure.

Months of planning drifted up to the rafters in a plume of smoke.

"Well," Mr. Easton said. "I hope you kids did a better job preparing than West Valley."

We watched as West Valley Middle School's robotics team sorted through their wreckage like investigators on the scene of a plane crash.

So far, every school in the competition had failed spectacularly. The gym was a graveyard of e-waste and splattered soup.

We had come back to LBJ the previous Monday, one week after Pyrite Days. Vice Principal Hopper's expulsion was "obsolete," according to my mom, since it was based on criminal charges that no longer existed. I overheard her on the phone with him before the decision was made to let us return. She said, "This way there's no more damage to the boys." She used the word "damage" repeatedly during the conversation, which sounded weird to me.

"That's a legal term," Pratchett said later. "She was reminding Hopper that they could sue his pants off for letting an evil cop ruin our lives at his school."

I didn't think my parents would ever sue the school. They were just using that threat as leverage. But it felt good to know they were fighting for me.

They didn't have much choice. True North Academy for Excellence had closed the previous Tuesday. Apparently, packages had been mailed anonymously to the Rust County supervisors, the police, and the local TV stations. They contained evidence of child-labor-law violations and the destruction of public documents.

I won't say who copied the evidence, but I will say that Jared's dad's printer is way low on toner.

At the same time, the school board members who had been in cahoots with Mr. Dekker and Officer Jim resigned, and the remaining members voted to reinstate Mr. Easton effective immediately. After the vote, the board president made a statement from the steps of city hall. "There's no good way to say it: this board failed one of our most beloved teachers, as well as his students. But today we took steps to make it right. We welcome Lawrence Easton back to the classroom and wish him the brightest of futures."

As for the park, Mr. Easton and Mayor Karl held a news conference announcing that our science teacher—a true Birdwell and the rightful heir to the land—had agreed to give up any claim on it. His only condition was that the city quickly extract the gold under the surface and return the land to use as a park as soon as possible.

All money generated from the gold would go directly to the school district.

Mr. Easton returned to school the same day we did. I had heard he would be there, but still, when I walked into Room 302, I couldn't hide my surprise at seeing him at the head of the class and all of Beef Squad on their regular stools. Karla Woo included.

I guess Mr. Hopper was serious about undoing the damage.

The bell rang.

"Where were we?" Mr. Easton said in his oatmeal-colored sweater. "Ah, yes. We had just taken a test on energy, when a certain grown-up did an incredibly stupid thing out in the parking lot. Who was *that* idiot?"

We all laughed.

He was back.

But with only five days till the competition, we couldn't make any major robotics changes. We had to rely on Karla's work from before we were expelled.

It was LBJ's turn to host the meet, so Saturday morning all of our parents came early to help set up tables and tape extension cords to the gym floor.

They were in the bleachers—the top row, with the best view. They stood and clapped when the judge announced our team.

The cheers were louder than I expected. Only then did I notice all the kids in the stands—our classmates. Normally the only kids you saw at a robotics competition were a few bored siblings. Our criminal reputation wasn't good for much, but I guess it was good enough to bring a crowd of spectators to this unspectacular event. Jesse and the skaters were there. Curtis Wannamaker and Maddie Harmon were a few rows back with some other kids from science class. And way in back, not far from our parents, sat Eric Bullock, Roger Denton, and—yes—Scott Dekker.

It had been a rough couple of weeks for Scott. Mr. Dekker

was out on bail, wearing an ankle bracelet that would alert the cops if he left Leonardville. Officer Jim was still behind bars. Maybe he couldn't afford the bond.

The news stories made it clear they could go to prison. I couldn't imagine how awful that must have been for Scott.

I did have an idea why he was here. Detective Ramirez had brought us a one-page proposal. It said that in consideration for the police dropping all charges against us, we would offer assistance in the prosecution of the two men arrested "and any accomplice(s) yet to be named."

There was only one person that could have been: the kid who'd conspired with them to lure us into Butte Nuggets Hall: Scott Dekker.

After talking it over, first with each other, then with our parents, we all signed the document, but with one change. It looked like this:

. . . ~~and any accomplice(s) yet to be named.~~

Maybe Scott knew why his legal problems had suddenly evaporated. Or maybe he'd decided to come to school that day for the same reason we'd decided not to send him to juvie.

Because seventh grade was tough enough without us kids making it tougher.

"Time to show these people whatcha got," Mr. Easton said. "Unless, of course, you don't have jack squat. Which, frankly, wouldn't surprise me."

Jared finished his final checks on the robot arm and

adjusted the position of the soup can, then leaned over the keyboard and typed "execute." His finger hovered over the return button. He froze.

"Come on," Karla said. "Let's win this thing and go play *Dynamus*."

With Karla on our *Dynamus* team—playing fair this time—Beef Squad had become a legit threat. We posted a top-ten score on Prudean Cellar Bug Hunt. UnicornKisses gave us a shout-out on one of his Friday videos.

But Jared still wasn't moving.

"Uh-oh," Mr. Easton said. "Our friend Jared is suffering from what medical doctors call a brain fart."

Jared stepped back from the table.

"Karla should do it," he said.

"Dude," she said, waving him off.

"No, you did all the work," Pratchett said. "It's only right."

"That's right," Hogue said. "I forgot we were even *on* Robotics Team."

She looked at me. I nodded.

As Karla stepped forward, another cheer rose from the bleachers. She looked back at us, and we were all smiling. She looked up to her parents back along the wall. Her expression was neither frightened nor cocky. It was the look of a girl who knew every single line of code she was about to execute, because she'd written it.

With a keystroke, she set the arm in motion.

ACKNOWLEDGMENTS

You know the sequence in every sports movie where the idiotic rookie fails over and over again while the coach patiently teaches them the fundamentals? I promise you, so does this book's editor, Beverly Horowitz.

There's an old joke that carving a sculpture is simple; you just chip off everything that doesn't look like a horse. I had some very unhorselike ideas for this book until my agent, Richard Abate, talked me into chipping them off.

My hilarious son, Mercer, and his friends served as the spiritual model for Beef Squad. I've never worried less about what a gang of boys was up to. A special mention goes to Hart Campbell (2005–2019), who lost his life to a drunk driver. Hart's humor and gentle self-possession helped me to write the character of Hogue. Any light seen there is his.

My daughter, Josie, lent her substantial attention to an early draft. Her notes pointed the way and her laughs buoyed my spirits.

On that topic, I never would have done this if Josh Lieb hadn't rudely written a book that made my kids laugh harder than they did at my jokes. Let us not speak his name again. Hey, stop it!

The character of Karla is brilliant, stylish, and protective of herself and her friends. Just like the real-life Karla Liu.

I started this book writing about my son's friends; I finished it writing about mine. Once again, Chris Motta and Mark Musco came through for me.

I thank my wife, Nicole Revere, for absolutely everything.

ABOUT THE AUTHOR

JASON ROSS is the winner of seven Primetime
Emmy Awards. He has co-authored two bestselling comedy
books and written for *The Daily Show with Jon Stewart* and
The Tonight Show Starring Jimmy Fallon, among others.
Jason grew up in Chico, California, where springtime starts
in February and the sidewalk cracks are just the right height
for skateboard tricks. He lives with his family in Los Angeles,
where it's springtime all year, and he still skateboards when
no one's looking. *The Amazing Beef Squad* is his debut novel.

JasonRoss.net